HOLDING THE THREADS

HOLDING THE THREADS

Alison Jesson

Matador
9 Priory Business Park,
Wistow Road, Kibworth Beauchamp,
Leicestershire. LE8 0RX
Tel: 0116 279 2299
Email: books@troubador.co.uk
Web: www.troubador.co.uk/matador
Twitter: @matadorbooks

ISBN: 978 1788035 699

British Library Cataloguing in Publication Data.
A catalogue record for this book is available from the British Library.

Printed and bound by CPI Group (UK) Ltd, Croydon, CR0 4YY
Typeset in 12 Sabon MT by Troubador Publishing Ltd, Leicester, UK

Matador is an imprint of Troubador Publishing Ltd

For my family,
past, present and future

Alison's first novel, *The Mind's Garden*, was published by Matador in 2012 and was very well received. She has also had poems published in leading poetry magazines and was shortlisted for the Hamish Canham poetry prize in 2006. Having previously worked as a psychotherapist, she is now retired.

MRS. McNAIRN.

· CHAPTER 1

SS Orita, Liverpool, UK to Lima, Peru. Somewhere in the Atlantic. Autumn 1904.

The rolling greyness stretched towards the horizon only to merge with an even greyer sky. I shivered and pulled my thin coat around me. I had not seen land for weeks. Everything I had ever known was behind me and I had only the vaguest idea about where I was going. What if I had made an awful mistake?

As the *Orita* rose and dipped through the waves, I closed my eyes and tried to let myself become part of the ship's movement. I felt trapped; there would be no turning back. Salt spray pricked my cheeks; my legs wobbled; my stomach churned. I gulped fresh air as if it were rationed.

To begin with, the voyage had seemed so exciting. There had been life-boat drills and instructions concerning the rules of the ship and the daily routine. There were other travellers to chat to and crew members to watch as they bustled about their duties. I often got lost in the maze of corridors below deck but it didn't seem to matter. Several other passengers were as confused as I, and we laughed together as we each stumbled back to our own cabins.

And in my cabin, waiting for me was my new husband, Arthur Stuart McNairn, or "Mac" as everyone called him.

Although the sea had been quite choppy while we crossed the Bay of Biscay, it had seemed quite funny to totter about the deck, clutching each other like drunkards. But now, after ten days confined to our cabin, as the ship had rolled and pitched in the Atlantic storm, I felt so feeble I couldn't imagine how I would endure almost another month at sea before we would finally set foot on dry land in Peru.

While I was undertaking my midwifery training at Doric Lodge, I had developed a pretty strong stomach, but the seasickness was relentless. We had been married just two weeks before we set sail and there were quite enough other physical experiences to cope with, without having to feel so vulnerable and exposed, as I vomited repeatedly into the chamber pot, which poor Mac had to dutifully empty. He was unaffected and had done his best to comfort me and plead with me to try and eat something, but I was so embarrassed by how I must have smelt in the stuffy stench of the cabin, I begged him to leave me alone.

I was clutching the railing while struggling to keep my hat from being snatched by the wind, when I was startled by an arm around my shoulders.

'How are you feeling, Beatrice?' Mac gazed down at me. He wore his thick woollen greatcoat, a tartan scarf and a black felt hat. 'You do look awfully pale. You really must try and eat something today. Come, let's see what there is for lunch.'

'Yes, I promise I will. I do feel much better, but let me just stay on deck for a few more moments while I finally take charge of my sea-legs. I'm sorry that I have been such a burden to you over these past days.'

'Don't be silly. That's what I'm here for. After all I did just promise you, "in sickness and in health". I think it was much worse for you than it was for me.'

I looked up at him. Such kind eyes. I have married a good man, I thought. Papa would have been so proud of me. My fellow trainees had teased me endlessly when they noticed that the good-looking McNairn was courting me. Mac was thought to be the best catch of all the men at Harley College, the interdenominational missionary training school in East London. He looked like a proper gentleman, well-dressed, tall, and clean shaven apart from his handlebar moustache which turned up at the ends like an enormous smile. He had a strong Edinburgh accent which endeared him to many.

The curriculum at Harley College had been extremely comprehensive. It included in-depth study of the Old and New Testaments, English language and literature, rhetoric, logic, psychology, ethics, Greek, apologetics, theology, and the art of writing and preaching sermons. In addition, health management and pharmacology were offered, and medical training was provided in local hospitals. With the schedule of lectures, prayer meetings and work activities which kept both of us busy and apart during the week, the only times we had spent together were at the weekend socials. Students came from all over the world and were expected to minister abroad at the end of the training. The authorities, while strongly encouraging the men to sort themselves out with wives before they travelled, offered them little opportunity to meet suitable women. Of necessity, our courtship was very short.

I was the only unmarried member of my family. I never knew my mother; she had died giving birth to Susannah, her thirteenth child, when I was barely fourteen months old. Papa had been devoted to his wife and had become very religious after her death. We lived quite comfortably in a large house in Hampton, Middlesex and Papa travelled every day to his work in Bond Street. Growing up in such a large family, as well as nannies and governesses, I seldom felt lonely. But in 1894, just before my nineteenth birthday, my comfortable life unravelled when Papa suddenly died. My older brothers and sisters were all married by then, and although Susannah and I remained living together in the family house with my older brother, Sidney, felt a loneliness that nothing could soothe. Further tragedy came when two of my older sisters, Evelyn and Lilian, as well as Sidney's twin brother, Gordon, also died; all within a couple of years. Lilian was only four years older than me and I had looked up to her all my life; I thought she was very wise. My grief felt so vast. The only way I could cope was to keep as busy as I could, running the Sunday school and visiting the sick in the parish. I was never out of mourning dress, and with few opportunities to socialise, I just assumed that I would probably never marry and I would have to join the world of sad spinsters. The final shock came when Susannah and Sidney each became engaged. I felt abandoned by everyone.

But one evening at church, I heard an elderly gentleman, called Sebastian Rutherford, give an enthusiastic address about his pastoral work in the Congo. He inspired me to think that perhaps I, too, could have a calling for missionary work. He spoke of the high death rate of both mothers and babies due to the lack of sanitation and poverty and the real need for trained nurses to go abroad and help save these poor souls.

With nine nieces and nephews, I reckoned that I already had plenty experience of pregnant women and babies, and the next day I made the bold decision to train to be a missionary midwife and go to Africa. Charles, my oldest brother, who had assumed the role of head of the family when Papa died, while praising my religious zeal, tried hard to dissuade me from going into "some dreadful jungle in nowhere land". But I was determined to do something with my life and not end up as some pathetic spinster earning my living as a teacher or a governess. Although the training was arduous and quite unlike anything I had come across in my sheltered childhood, I gradually began to enjoy assisting the poorest of women from the filthiest of slums to bring new souls into the world. At last I felt worthwhile.

But Mac discovered he was to be sent to Peru. He was to take the place of Will Newell who had recently died of typhoid. When he asked me to accompany him as his wife, I was so surprised I agreed without thinking about my own plans for a life in the Congo or about what it would really involve. And while I felt so seasick during the storm that had hurled the ship in and out of the waves, I wondered what conceit had made me believe that I would even make a good missionary's wife in Cuzco, a town in Peru, where English missionaries had previously been persecuted? Although Mac had been learning Spanish and seemed to have a good grasp of the language already, I knew only the few dozen words he had taught me. And neither of us spoke Quechua, the language of the Andean Indians to whom we were hoping to minister.

'Goodness, you are freezing,' he said as he held my hands in his. 'How long have you been standing out here?' He took me firmly by the arm and led me to the dining room. I managed some soup and a couple of slices of bread and butter. I began to thaw.

That night, after we had knelt to say our prayers I lay in his arms and asked him to tell me the story of the Incas again. I knew that he loved to relate the Inca tales. He kissed my cheek gently and began.

'Well, let me see now. You remember it all started with Manco Capac and his brothers who emerged from three great windows in the mountains. They were tasked by Inti, the sun god, to find a spot where the gold sceptre, which he had entrusted to them, would sink with ease into the ground. They were to bring their ancient wisdom and civilizing arts to the rude and scattered peoples inhabiting the mountain lands. But Manco, the conqueror, eliminated his brothers one after the other, and with his sister-wife, Mama Ocillo, he taught and guided the Indian tribes in the paths of old wisdom and gradually knitted them together into some semblance of unity. Finally, he arrived in the beautiful valley of Huatenay where he founded the city of Cuzco, which became the "navel", the capital of the great Inca Empire.' Mac stroked my hair and looked intently at me. 'And that, my dearest, is where we are going to live, in the City of the Sun, and where together we will spread the word of Christ and help the poor citizens break away from the corrupt rule of the Catholic church.'

'Oh Mac, it does sound so exciting but I am finding it

so hard to visualise what our life will be like. How am I going to be any use to you until I can speak their language and learn their ways and what if they won't let us stay?' Up until now, I hadn't let him see how anxious I was.

He pulled himself away from me and sat up. 'Come, come Beatrice. That's no way to talk. You know that it is God's wish that we are being sent there and therefore He will take care of us,' he said firmly.

'I'm sorry dearest. You're right. I'm just being silly. Take no notice and go back to the story.'

'Well, as long as you don't interrupt,' he teased. 'So, where was I? Well, the Inca Empire expanded rapidly in the early 1400s. They either conquered anyone who resisted them or made peaceful negotiations with groups who agreed to come under their rule. Under the Incas the arts and sciences flourished. They constructed terraces all over the mountain slopes in order to grow crops and they irrigated the deserts by a complex system of aqueducts so that they could grow fields of vegetables and grains. They built vast storehouses so that no one ever starved and they created fortresses, temples and palaces, fitting immense blocks of stone together as never seen before. Although there was a hierarchy, everything was communally organized and everyone was fed and clothed. Three fundamental laws lay at the root of the Empire's prosperity; *ama suya*: Thou shalt not lie; *ama llulla*: thou shalt not steal; *ama kella*: thou shalt not be idle. But then, four hundred years ago, came Pizarro, and the Spanish, who tore down the golden image of the sun, slaughtered the Inca leaders and in the name of Romanism turned the people into slaves.'

But I heard no more as I had drifted off to sleep.

CHAPTER 2

At Sea. Autumn 1904.

I lay back on my steamer chair and closed my eyes against the sun. My Spanish phrase book lay unopened on my lap. We had found a relatively sheltered spot on deck and hoped not to be interrupted by other passengers while we relaxed and digested the steak and kidney pie we had eaten for lunch.

'I think my little impromptu service went rather well last evening, don't you agree?' asked Mac, looking up from his bible. 'Mrs Collins thanked me personally this morning.'

Several passengers had gathered round as he announced that he would hold a short service on the foredeck and we had sung hymns together and said prayers for a safe voyage. He had also preached a brief sermon based on St Paul's first letter to the Corinthians. Street preaching in the East End had been one of the activities that he had enjoyed the most at Harley College and he never minded who listened or who heckled. He was good at preaching and had a talent for memorising appropriate bible passages which he could use in the face of criticism. Preaching on board ship, he had a captive audience who were glad for anything that broke the monotony of the six-week voyage.

I reached out to squeeze his hand; I felt so proud of him. At last I had become used to the motion of the ship and I was back to my old self.

Although the College had encouraged the men to find themselves suitable wives, apparently, Mac had been almost as surprised as I, when he asked me to marry him and make the long journey to Peru. He knew very little about women or marriage; his own mother had died in '81, when he was just eight, leaving him and seven siblings, aged four months to seventeen years, to be brought up by a series of housekeepers. His father had never remarried and had spent most of his days cloistered in his artist's studio. Despite being united in their grief for their mother, as each of his siblings grew older, they seemed to drift away from him and Mac must have felt as if his family was forever disintegrating

Mac had been so engrossed in his studies at Harley College that he'd not really noticed any of us women trainees from Doric Lodge. It wasn't until one night when he heard some of his fellows talking quite disrespectfully about us and what sort of wives we'd make, that he realised he'd only ever seen women students as sort of sister figures. All except me. He thought that I had a beauty and sense of serenity about me that stood me apart from the others. 'I love your pale skin and the way you twist your beautiful dark hair into a neat little bun. You look like a delicate spring flower,' he told me on the day that he had proposed. I had blushed and was lost for words. No one had ever said anything about the way I looked, except occasionally,

9

Susannah, would tell me a button was undone, or my skirt looked rumpled.

Mac was anxious about snatching me away from my family to accompany him halfway round the world to Peru. He thought it might be unfair and that the rigours of missionary life might prove too much for me. But he also knew that I had a strong faith and a determination to continue the midwifery work I did with destitute families. I suggested to him that perhaps, since our childhood losses had been so similar, we could actually be very good for each other.

Each day we stood for a while as near to the bow of the ship as we were allowed and scanned the horizon for the first signs of the land of South America, even though it would take many more days at sea while we rounded Cape Horn. Unlike me, I knew that Mac felt confident and passionate about the work we were about to take up.

Ever since Pizarro had slaughtered the Inca rulers, the sword and the Cross had been invariably linked, but it was by the cruelty of the sword rather than the message of the Cross that Roman Catholicism had supplanted the Inca gods. Peru had suffered four centuries of priestly corruption. Nowadays, sins could be forgiven by buying an indulgence for a few pence, mumbling prayers before a saint's statue or by kissing the toe of some image. Mac had been shocked when he learnt that, as with other Catholic countries, bible reading in Peru was strongly discouraged. Some of the more sophisticated might be familiar with isolated texts from the Psalms and the Prophets but only if the words could be applied to the Virgin Mary. The Gospel stories and the teachings of Jesus were virtually unknown.

Many educated men had been driven away from the nonsense they heard preached, while the women remained doggedly obedient to the priest and the confessional, despite tales of young girls who were frequently defiled by that same priest. It was the loving Christ whom Mac had discovered when he was just fourteen that he wanted to bring to this land.

The first graduates of Harley College, Fred Peters and John Jarrett, had arrived in Cuzco in the late 1890s and had attempted to set up religious meetings and establish a Protestant church, but they were met with fury from the Catholic priests who stirred up the locals to stone them and expel them from the city. They narrowly escaped via the back streets under cover of darkness and fled to Lima. Poor John Jarrett was also suffering from smallpox at the time. Undaunted, they returned a year later and for a while they managed establish a small school. But once again the mob was incited by the priests to drive them out.

Eventually, Dr Henry Gratton Guinness, who had founded Harley College, visited Cuzco and was able to suggest a more organized but subtle attempt to establish a missionary presence. Following his advice, John Jarrett proceeded to set up a photographic studio offering portrait photography, and although initially the priests had forbidden anyone to patronize it, once the wealthier residents learnt that a certain Father Fernando had had his photograph taken there, they flocked to the shop which from then on became very successful. At the same time, Fred Peters taught himself the basics of carpentry and set up a cabinet making shop which employed several locals and Indians. Once the two businesses were established, the missionaries were able to hold meetings after work and gradually attracted a small following of converts. Other missionaries, including the Newells, joined them, though sadly Will Newell died of typhoid and his widow had returned to England.

But things were different now. The way had been paved, and with Mac's specialist medical knowledge and me as an additional midwife, our arrival was eagerly awaited. He had been donated a box of medicines and instruments by the supporters in Reading, and he felt confident that since many in Cuzco were in desperate need of medical care, he would be able to offer this, and at the same time he would tell them about their Saviour. In our trunk, Mac had packed as many bibles and pamphlets as he could squeeze in. Having set sail from Liverpool at the end of September 1904, we hoped we would be in Cuzco for Christmas; our first Christmas as a married couple.

I stared out to sea where small white horses caught the afternoon sun.

'A penny for your thoughts?' asked Mac

'Oh I don't think they are worth that much, dear. I was simply wondering what the family might be doing right now,' I replied, shifting myself to be able to look at him directly.

'Are you missing them so very much?'

'Yes I am. I was thinking about my nephews. I so miss cuddling them and little Richard and Ralph should both be walking by now.'

'Well, it won't be long now Beatrice, before you'll be cuddling plenty of bonny wee babies that you have helped to bring into the world.'

'That's as may be, but not until I have mastered both the Spanish and Quecha for "Push" and "Stop Pushing",' I laughed waving my phrasebook.

'Beatrice. Look!' Mac pointed towards the horizon where a shaft of bright sunlight was spilling out from behind a puffy white cloud. 'It reminds me of the beautiful stained glass Ascension window at St Giles Cathedral in Edinburgh. I designed a similar one for a church in St Andrews.'

'Tell me more about how you started designing stained glass,' I asked. It seemed silly that there were still so many things I didn't know about my husband.

'Well, I suppose it all came about after my "road to Damascus" moment. Religion had not been part of our family life except for George, my older brother, who always accompanied Miss Finlay, the housekeeper, to church on Sundays. George often used to sit on the back steps in the evening sun and read from his bible in an annoyingly loud voice. I was forever yelling at him to shut up, until one evening, when I was fourteen, I heard George reading that wonderful verse from St John's gospel over and over again. *"For God so loved the world that he gave his only begotten Son, that whosoever believeth in him should not perish, but have everlasting life."'* Mac sat up and looked directly at me.

'It was most peculiar. Something inside me lurched. I stepped outside the back door and looked across the garden. As I repeated the phrase to myself, for just a few moments, I felt as if I was floating, weightless, looking down on the garden and the row of houses. Suddenly, I realised that God had actually spoken to me. I was filled with a love and a longing I had never experienced before. It was quite incredible.' He fell silent.

'Go on,' I said.

'Well, very quietly, I sat down on the steps next to George and asked, "Will you read me some more of that?" From that moment on my life began again. I went with George to the United Presbyterian church, attended religious meetings and for a while thought seriously about training for the priesthood. My father thought I was mad. He'd been quite withdrawn for much of my childhood, but he saw my talent for drawing and was very keen for me to become a landscape artist like himself. Of course, money was short, but I managed to find a way of combining both my love of God with my talent for art.' Mac paused for a moment and looked back out over the waves.

'So, when I was fifteen I became an apprentice and then a draughtsman with a stained glass firm of Ballantine and Gardiner, who had designed several of the windows in the cathedral. The vibrant colours of stained glass had always entranced me and I even won an award for one of my designs. It was during my apprenticeship that I first heard Henry Gratton Guinness preaching and I decided that once I had saved up enough money I would train to be a missionary.' He pointed again towards the horizon.

'When I look at how the light catches that vast expanse of sea, I imagine all the variations of blues and greens I would use to make a window to represent Christ walking on the Sea of Galilee.'

'Perhaps one day I'll see all the windows you've made,' I said, and I felt a rush of love for him. We both fell silent for a while and then, after I had flicked through my phrase book a few times I stood up and asked,

'*Buenas tardes, querido esposo, ¿Cómo estas? Te gustaría una taza de te*? That is meant to be, "Good afternoon, dearest husband. How are you? Would you like a cup of tea." Did I say it right?'

Mac laughed. 'Just perfect, my dear. Let us go and partake!'

CHAPTER 3

Peru. Autumn 1904.

Sunlight flooded the room as I opened the shutters and looked down at a bustling plaza. In the centre was a fountain surrounded by marble seats on which some small children were playing. On rough cobbles around the edges of the square, under covered awnings, sat both men and women with their wares spread out before them: pretty ribbons, slabs of meat, loaves of bread, heaps of oranges, yellow bananas, multi-coloured corn cobs, and what looked like piles of rusty potatoes. A blur of reds and greens and blues and browns.

'Oh Mac, do come and look.'

Mac groaned, but rubbing the sleep from his eyes, he emerged from a tangle of bed-clothes to join me at the window. Immediately below us an Indian man was shouting and pulling on the reins of a mule who was attempting to eat a bundle of alfalfa which was hanging from an awning. He wore dirty, torn trousers and a poncho woven in rainbow patterns of green, red and blue. A woman, whose alfalfa the mule was attempting to steal, was yelling back at him. She seemed to be wearing an enormous number of brightly dyed skirts, each one tied a little higher than the preceding one. On her head was a strange looking grass hat covered with navy cloth with a wide red brim.

'Oh Beatrice, we are here at last,' Mac hugged me. 'This is the South America I have been dreaming of – the starting point of our mission.' His arm swept over the vista before us.

The *Orissa* had finally docked at Callao, the port for Lima, in late afternoon on the previous day. Throughout the remainder of our voyage the ship had called at several ports: Lourenco Marques in Brazil, Buenos Aires, Santiago and La Paz. Each time I'd said a wistful goodbye to fellow passengers with whom I'd enjoyed many hours of conversation. Here, the dockside bustled with people, baggage, mules and carts; it took nearly an hour for us to be reunited with our suitcases and the large trunk which were piled in a heap beside us. Small boys surrounded us, pulled at our sleeves, babbled in a language I could not understand and pointed towards what was presumably a hotel. I felt quite alarmed and clutched hold of Mac's sleeve. Mac appeared unruffled and selecting the tallest of the boys, who wore what appeared to be a garish, knitted nightcap on his head, said firmly, '¡*Llévanos al Hotel La Posada por favor*!'

The boy snapped his fingers, instructed three much smaller boys to pick up the luggage and gesturing to us to follow, cried, '¡*Sigueme Señor*!'

'But Mac, how do you know we can trust him?'

'Don't worry my dear. Captain Forster knows this place well and last night he gave me some very useful tips about arriving at Callao. He also recommended a reasonable hotel nearby.'

We must have made a peculiar sight; a lanky boy in a woollen cap, bearing a large suitcase on his shoulders, followed by a tall white man in a long black coat and felt hat, and a woman gripping his coat sleeve, trying to keep up, trailed by three small boys manhandling a large trunk and another smaller suitcase. Eventually we arrived at the hotel situated on a large open plaza. I felt quite giddy as I walked, as if the dusty street was the swaying deck of the steamer from which I had just disembarked.

For supper we were offered some soup, so full of peppers it set my mouth on fire, followed by a plate of small knobbly potatoes. After we had eaten, we retired to our room and fell into bed without having unpacked a thing. We both slept solidly until the light and loud voices brought me to the window.

After breakfast we wandered around the town, taking in everything we saw. It was all so new and exciting. The streets and alleyways jostled with noise and colour; Indians in bright-hued ponchos and shawls led reluctant mules; children ran in and out of doorways; old women in what appeared to be bowler hats gossiped in corners; both monks and nuns in black or brown robes, each bearing large crucifixes on cords around their necks went in and out of the numerous churches. We kept pointing out sights to each other and exclaiming our amazement. In the afternoon we took an electric car for the six mile trip into the capital city, Lima, the "City of the Kings". From June to mid-November the capital is normally swathed in mist, but on that day the streets and plazas were flooded with bright sunshine. The city was very elegant; large houses painted blue or yellow opened onto courtyards filled with flowers; ornate churches were decorated in the Renaissance style and a great plaza was bisected by long avenues which were lined with trees and flowers. After so many weeks at sea, I felt inspired by the beauty of it, and compared to the colourless, bleak East End of London in which I had spent so much time in my training, this city felt magnificent.

'I think I am going to like Peru very much,' I announced, taking Mac's arm.

'I'm so glad, dearest. Let's hope the Peruvians like us just as much.'

Two days later we boarded another ship which took three days to land us at Mollendo, a port in the south of Peru. Here we would take a train for the next stage of the journey. Having so enjoyed being able to walk around without having to hold onto walls or railings, I hoped I wouldn't become seasick again. But the small ship hugged the shoreline and the sea was calm. While we gazed at the landscape slipping by, much to my amusement, Mac read out loud from a badly translated guidebook.

"*Peru has three distinct regions for the visitor. We have our coast strip of desert which can run for some 1,400 miles along the shore of the Pacifico Sea. From this you will rise into the mountains which we call the Sierra, a region of fertile hills and valleys lying between the east and west ranges of the Andes. Here you will find many high altitudes of between 9,000 and 12,000 feet, and including the Punas, our vast mountain wastes from which the giant peaks rise to over 20,000 feet. Visitors may be affected by soroche if they are not used to our high altitudes. From the tops of the east range the mountains descend quickly away to the Montaña, our densely wooded region of valleys which merge into the jungles of the great Amazon River.*"

We both laughed at the description but as the sky behind the distant mountains flushed with pink, rose and then indigo blackness, dotted with millions of stars, we fell silent. I felt supremely privileged to have been allowed to travel to this amazing country.

'Let us praise God for bringing us to this magical place,' said Mac.

Just after dawn we disembarked at Mollendo, and this involved sitting in huge baskets that swung from the ship's derricks into launches waiting below in the swirling waves. I felt very frightened and kept my eyes tight shut until I could feel myself on solid ground once more. We left Mollendo that same day on a train so crowded that we were only just able to find seats where we could also keep an eye on our luggage. The train took nearly six hours, slowly climbing from sea level all the way up to Arequipa. At first, we passed the great expanse of crescent-shaped sand dunes, which we had read about, as we chugged towards the lower hills of the Andes. Then the track began to twist and turn so that the view was forever changing; one minute a craggy rock face, the next a view of a distant snow-capped mountain peak. We stopped several times at small settlements and peasant women clambered onto the train with baskets of fruit for sale. We arrived in Arequipa at dusk, just as the last rays of the sun glowed over the volcano, El Misti, which towered above the town.

This arrival time I felt more confident and I waited on the platform surrounded by our luggage and the inevitable small boys who tugged at my coat sleeve, while Mac strode off to find someone to help us. To my surprise, he returned accompanied by an English man, perhaps a few years younger than him, who smiled broadly and held out his hand.

'Thomas Payne. I am so pleased to meet you, Mrs McNairn. At last you are safely here. I hope you are not too tired by your arduous journey.' He was nearly as tall as Mac but he had a heavier build. His face was tanned and his dark hair looked rather in need of a trim. He grasped my hand in a firm handshake and held my gaze with his dark brown eyes for a fraction longer than I expected.

'No, no, not at all Mr Payne. I am delighted to meet you as well. I had no idea that anyone was going to greet us before we got to Cuzco.'

'Well, I knew when your ship was due to arrive in Callao and since I had some business to attend to in Arequipa, I thought that once I had finished I would simply meet the train every day until you arrived. And here you both are!'

He seized both our suitcases, gestured to two boys to carry the trunk and led the way to a small hotel next to the station.

In reality, I was exhausted and would have gladly tumbled into bed, but not wanting to miss anything or appear rude, after splashing my face with cold water and pinning my hair, I joined the men in the cramped hotel dining room where we ate some sort of vegetable broth served with small potatoes.

'It's really good to have you both here in Peru. Our numbers are still small and we have so much work to do,' said Tom Payne, as he pushed his plate away. 'Mr and Mrs Peters and the Jarretts are so pleased that you both have some medical training as it has become clear that this is one of the most important ways to win over hearts and minds.'

'You clearly speak Spanish so fluently, Mr Payne. Did it take you long to learn?' I asked.

'I've been in Peru for just a couple of years. First I was in Lima which is where I learnt the basics of the language, but since the start of this year, I have been helping the Jarretts set up regular bible study classes where we have to speak a mixture of Spanish and Quechua, if we have any hope of reaching out to the Indians.'

'I hope I can master all the words I am going to need to help the women when they are in labour.'

'I am sure it won't take you long, Mrs McNairn, and I can assure you that Mrs Jarrett and Mrs Peters will very happily assist.'

'Can you tell us a wee bit more about the people to whom we will be ministering,' asked Mac. 'We saw so many different sorts of folk in Lima, from well-dressed men and ladies in fine silks and mantillas to scruffy peasants in ponchos and woolly trousers. What can we expect in Cuzco?'

'Well, Cuzco is quite different to Lima. I think the population is something like 19,000 – half of whom are *Mestizos* or *Cholos* – half-breeds who have both Spanish and Incan blood. They speak a mixture of Quechua and Spanish. Then there are the *Blancos* or white Spanish speakers, and the remainder are poor, uneducated Indians, who only speak Quechua. After the 1782 rebellion by Indians and *Mestizos*, the Quechua language was banned, but there was quite a revival of it after Peru gained independence almost 100 years ago, and now it is spoken by many.'

'I have been studying Spanish since I knew I was going to be sent to Peru, but my poor wife is going to need a bit of help and our grasp of Quechua is negligible. We will have to find a good teacher, won't we Beatrice?'

Suddenly I felt very tired and rather overwhelmed by the enormity of the task ahead. What would Papa have thought if he could see me now? Would he have approved of this venture or would he have begged me to be sensible and to settle down safely in England? But I also felt excited; I was going to be doing something that was worthwhile and although the task would be challenging, I was determined to make a success of it. I heard the scraping of a chair on the floor as Mac rose to his feet and realising that I hadn't been paying attention, I flushed. Both Mac and Mr Payne were staring at me.

'I thank you, Mr Payne, for your warm welcome, but I think it is high time this one got some sleep,' said Mac cheerfully.

'Of course, of course, I shouldn't have chattered away for so long. Tomorrow, I will give you both a guided tour of this lovely city.'

The following morning Tom Payne led us through the streets of Arequipa. Stone houses, painted in hues of rose, cream and harebell blue glowed in the morning sunshine. Through archways we could see small patios filled with flowers and looking up at the balconies I caught glimpses of young women wearing gorgeous silks, their hair adorned with lace mantillas. But by contrast, in street corners and dark doorways I saw both men, women and children, dressed in rags, holding out their hands for alms. One small girl, no more than about four years old, covered in sores, tugged at my skirt, and in turn, I tugged at Mr Payne's sleeve to ask if he had any spare coins.

'Every Saturday is known as "Beggars' Day" in Arequipa,' Payne explained, as he slipped some change into the child's hand. 'Giving money to the poor is seen by the upper- classes as a worthy and charitable act and it costs them very little to spare a few coins. The city is well known for being very religious but it is all just for show. This so-called charity doesn't even scratch the surface. It really sickens me. The old or incapable are just left to die with no support or medical help.'

'But doesn't the Church do anything for them?' I asked as we walked on.

'Unfortunately not. The Church and the priests are the worst. The Indians are generally regarded as too ignorant to be worth bothering about and the rich use them as slaves who can be bought and sold. Virtue does not consist of being good or doing good deeds but in the punctilious attendance at religious ceremonies. You will soon discover that all the Catholic church provides is ceremonies, candles, incense, rituals, and feast days with exotic processions and fireworks. Women especially, who have little else to interest them, only attend early morning mass to discuss the latest scandals or to hear a fresh supply of gossip. Sundays are seen as an opportunity to parade up and down in their latest dresses and finery. And, as I think you know, the bible is forbidden because it is believed that the gospels contain blasphemies against the Virgin and that they have been mistranslated and could undermine the very foundation of the Church.'

'I see what you mean about the amount of work we have ahead of us,' said Mac as we came to a halt outside a church. 'I understand now how hard it must have been for the Jarretts and Peters when they first arrived in Peru and the persecution they suffered.'

We had threaded our way through many streets and arrived at the central plaza. One side was taken up by a vast twin-towered cathedral built from the white sillar rock which had once spewed out of the volcano, El Misti. The centre of the plaza was laid out like an English garden with lawns and low hedges surrounding an impressive fountain but it was also filled with lush green palm trees. Such a contrast, I thought, between the beauty and grace of this plaza and the squalor and poverty I had seen in some of the back streets. The difference between rich and poor couldn't have been more marked.

Mr Payne seemed quite charming. His sometimes serious nature was balanced by his sense of humour and his enthusiasm for the work. I liked him immediately. Why was such a pleasant young man unmarried? He had smartly side-stepped any questions I had posed about his family and origins. What was his story?

CHAPTER 4

Peru 1904

Two days later, on a damp misty morning, the three of us and all our luggage clambered onto the train for Cuzco. Mac and I both felt weary and impatient for the endless journey to be over. I could tell that Mac liked Tom Payne and imagined they would work well together. I hoped that the other missionaries in Cuzco would appreciate all the skills he had to offer. Out of the train window, initially all we could see were fields of alfalfa and maize, but as the gradient increased, the train emerged into radiant sunshine at Pampa de Arrieros. From there the mountains rose higher and higher until they reached a large plain covered with low stubby pasture. There we saw the strangest looking animals, not quite sheep, but also not goats.

'Those are alpacas,' Payne explained. 'They are used solely for their soft wool, whereas the llamas, of which you will see plenty more, are used as pack animals.'

Soon we were crossing a snow plain and I began to feel distinctly unwell. I felt breathless and had the beginnings of a headache. Mac looked at me with alarm. 'I'm all right,' I protested weakly, 'just a little breathless in here with all the cigarette smoke.'

'Don't worry, Mrs McNairn. We are the highest point now. This is Crucere Alto and we are over 14,500 feet above sea level. Most people suffer from a touch of *soroche*, or altitude sickness, when they first arrive, but you will both acclimatize over the next few days.'

Although Mac had done some mountain walking in Scotland in his youth he was amazed by the huge gradients of this landscape. As for me, the highest hill I had ever encountered was Box Hill in Surrey. Far below were small wispy clouds as well as miles of craggy mountain tops. Gradually the train snaked back down towards green fields and the shores of Lake Titicaca and I began to feel slightly better. After one night in the small hotel in Juliaca, we travelled north again until we reached La Raya, where Mr Payne pointed out a tiny stream trickling over the rocks near the rail track.

'This little stream is called the Vilcamayu or "Urubamba" which in Quechua means "sacred river" and eventually, when it has been joined by many other streams and rivers, it will become the "Mighty Amazon". It was here in this very valley that the Incas chose to settle. They terraced the hillsides, cultivated the soil, and built their strongholds and palaces, and still today you will see many small Indian villages scattered along its course.'

'It is truly beautiful,' said Mac, gazing far down into the valley below, carpeted with fields of green barley and yellow maize.

'You should see it at the end of the wet season in February

when this little stream becomes a rushing torrent,' replied Payne.

Finally, the train halted at Checacupe. 'This is the end of the line I'm afraid,' said Payne. 'We spend one more night here and tomorrow, first thing, we make the rest of the journey to Cuzco by stagecoach.'

I was exhausted. Exciting as the train ride had been, I couldn't believe that we still had such a long way to go. Cuzco must be at the ends of the earth. I felt dirty and dusty. Strands of my unravelled hair clung to my damp forehead. I had a thumping headache from the altitude but I was too scared to say anything as I knew my irritation might burst out as rudeness. But Mac, bless him, even though he was clearly as tired as I, took a deep breath, gave Payne a beaming smile and said to me,

'Come my dear. Let us rest now. Surely the Lord will give us the strength for this final chapter.'

The following day, after many hours of bumping, lurching, stopping and starting, along precipitous mountain roads, in a carriage drawn by eight obstreperous mules, we finally came to a bend in the dirt track and caught our first glimpse of Cuzco spread out before us in the valley below. A maze of terracotta roofs glowed in the evening sun.

'They say that Cuzco was laid out by the Incas in the shape of a jaguar,' explained Mr Payne. 'You can't really see it properly as the light is failing now, but at one end was the fortress of Sacsayhuamán, which represented the teeth of the jaguar and the rest of its body was mapped out by the streets and other buildings. Sacsayhuamán was where the Inca ruler, Manco Inca, besieged Cuzco when it was occupied by the Spanish. The view from up there is tremendous, especially in the early morning.'

We looked to where Payne's finger was pointing.

'Since Pizarro's conquest,' Payne continued, 'it has changed shape dramatically. In Inca times the two rivers, the Tullumayo and the Huatenay, rushed through gorges on either side of the city. Each street in the city was built with a gulley down the centre and the rivers washed the city streets clean every day. However, eventually the rivers were canalised to prevent flooding and then the Spaniards built houses over them. Unfortunately, what we are left with today are rivers clogged with sewage, and possibly what no one has yet told you,' he glanced at me with a nervous smile. 'Cuzco is a very smelly city.'

'I think I can just about make out the cathedral. Whereabouts is the Sun Temple?' asked Mac.

'It's just a bit further southeast, but I will show it to you properly in the morning, when we all meet up and I introduce you to Mr and Mrs Jarrett.'

It was dark when we finally reached La Plaza del Regocijo and stopped outside the hotel where we would stay for the first few weeks until a suitable house could be rented. With a mixture of exhaustion and elation, we bid Tom Payne goodnight and after a quick supper, we collapsed into bed.

I woke to what was now becoming a symphony of familiar sounds: guttural cries of Indians attempting to hustle their donkeys across the plaza; a chorus of voices calling out wares for sale; gleeful shouts of children chasing each other around the narrow streets; jangling mule bells and sonorous church bells summoning the devoted to prayer.

Tom Payne called for us after breakfast. He looked fresh and energetic, whereas we both still felt rather washed-out and full of headache. To begin with, he led us through a maze of backstreets so that we could get a feel for the city. He was right; every street stank like an overflowing privy and I tried to hide how sick it made me feel.

He pointed out how the lower stories of many of the houses still showed the exquisite Inca masonry – massive blocks of beautifully worked stone fitted together so that not even a needle could slide between the blocks – and the upper stories of adobe mud bricks.

'There is a wonderful tale about how the Incas discovered that if they rubbed the dark red leaves of a certain plant onto stone, they could soften it to such an extent that it became like a paste, and that is how these huge blocks fitted together so well. Apparently, they learnt this trick by observing birds drilling holes into solid rock to carve out a nest using this same plant. Of course, this is one of many tales of the Inca magic, but since no one has come up with a better explanation, I rather like it.' He rubbed his hand over the stone wall.

Everywhere was sunshine, brilliant, intense sunshine. It reflected off the white walls of the Spanish houses and glowed on the red-tiled roofs that seemed to clamber up the green-brown mountains which surrounded the city.

'This is the famous Plaza de Armas, the centre of the Inca empire, or navel of the world,' explained Payne sweeping his arm around the entire square.

'So is this also the spot where Tupac Amaru was beheaded. I've read all about that,' said Mac. 'The poor man was only captured, Beatrice, because he refused to abandon his wife who was about to give birth.' I looked in wonder around the square. It was vast.

'That's right,' replied Payne. 'The Spanish then built this amazing cathedral on the same site as palace of Inca Wiracocha, using stones they pilfered from Sacsayhuamán. Shall we go inside?'

It was the first time we had been inside any sort of church since we had left England. Compared to the plain simple churches we were used to this cathedral was hugely ornate. It almost dripped with gold and silver and the walls were hung with many Renaissance paintings – one of which depicted the Last Supper where the main dish was a plump guinea pig!

'I can't decide if it is beautiful or hideous,' I said.

'Both,' laughed Payne. 'Come through here and I'll show you the precious crucifix. Apparently during the earthquake of 1650, the citizens processed around the Plaza with a crucifix, and prayed for the earthquake to stop, which miraculously, it did. The crucifix they carried is now called *El Señor de los Temblores* (The Lord of the Earthquakes). Every year in Holy Week they take it out and parade it all around the town. It's a huge event and everyone attends.

'But why is our Lord painted black?' asked Mac, pointing to the image in the alcove.

'Well, during the parade they throw *ñucchu* flowers at him – these are supposed to resemble droplets of blood and the wounds of crucifixion. The flowers leave a sticky residue and combined with the smoke from votive candles which are lit beneath the statue, he gets blacker every year.

Rumour has it that underneath that ridiculous embroidered skirt he is as white as you or me. But come now, it is time for us to meet up with the Jarretts and they will tell you more about our work and what it involves.'

The table was only big enough for five adults to squeeze round. The Jarrett's three older children sat on a bench set against the wall, balancing their soup bowls on their laps. A toddler sat in a high chair next to his mother who periodically offered him a spoonful from her own dish, in between talking to us and directing the other children to sit still and be quiet. I wasn't sure what the soup contained, only that it was very spicy and I longed for a cool glass of water to help wash it down.

John and Florence Jarrett had welcomed us when we arrived at their house after a short walk from the cathedral up several narrow streets. Their children swarmed around Tom Payne, asking if he had brought them anything. He grinned, rumpled their hair, and produced a package of toasted, sweetened corn from his pocket, which was immediately confiscated by Mrs Jarrett, with the promise of its return after lunch. The children were lined up and presented to us in turn.

'This is Nellie, who is seven. Next is Harry who is…'

'I'm six already' interrupted the boy, grubby faced with a huge smile.

'Harold, don't interrupt when I'm talking,' snapped his mother, 'and this is Kathleen who is four and Baby Johnny who is nearly two.' She gathered Johnny into her arms, kissed him fondly and waved his arm at me. The child squawked and wriggled to be put down. The two girls had matching pinafore frocks and the boy wore shorts and a white shirt. Clearly, they'd been dressed in their Sunday best for our arrival.

Florence Jarrett was a tall, skinny woman with a pointed chin and close-set eyes, giving her a rather fox-like look. I was surprised that after all the years she had spent in South America, she still had such a strong cockney accent. Her husband was quite a bit shorter, with brown hair swept over an obvious bald patch, a well-clipped moustache and gold rimmed spectacles which made him appear studious. I guessed that we were all about the same age and, from the moment we arrived at the house, it was clear that Mrs Jarrett wore the trousers.

The walls of the small room had been painted white and had a few pictures tacked onto them but the floor appeared to be hardened mud with a several strips of linoleum laid over it. At the further end of the room hung a bookshelf composed of three planks of wood held together with a strap and next to it were two wooden armchairs chairs with pretty cushions. Two doors led off the room, one to a tiny kitchen, the other to a staircase leading up to where I assumed there were bedrooms.

'If you need the lav, it's out the back. 'Fraid we have to share it with the other families, but it does well enough,' said Mrs Jarrett.

'What a lovely home you have Mrs Jarrett,' I said. 'You have made it look so nice. Have you lived here for long?' Actually, I didn't think the home was at all lovely. I was expecting something bigger and brighter and I couldn't imagine how the family managed in such a small space. Naturally I wasn't expecting anything like the house I'd grown up in as a child, but this seemed little better than some of the slum houses in London I'd visited during my training.

'We moved in 'ere just after Kathy was born. You should 'ave seen where we was before! We were all crammed into a room with a smelly wood-fired stove in the corner. This is much better. Once you've got a feel of Cuzco, we'll help you find just as nice a place for you and Mr McNairn. Don't you worry.'

I finished my soup and with my mouth still burning I asked for a glass of water. Nellie was dispatched to bring the water which was poured into a cup from a large jug standing in the corner. It was lukewarm.

'It's probably still a bit tepid, but you have to boil every scrap of water in this country, otherwise, who knows what germs are in it. That's what took poor Bob Newell. He got the typhoid. I don't know how he got it because Fanny was always ever so careful.' Mrs Jarrett wiped baby Johnny's mouth with a handkerchief. There was an awkward silence.

'Where do Mr and Mrs Peters live?' enquired Mac trying to change the topic from the death of the missionary we had come to replace.

'They are up the hill, a bit further towards Sacsayhuamán. They have a lovely view but we like to be here in the thick of things,' replied Mr Jarrett. 'You'll see them this evening when we all come together for prayers in the meeting room over the cabinet shop. Mr Peters and Mr Payne made all the furniture you see in this house. We have half a dozen *Mestizos* and Indians working in the shop now. It's going really well.'

When we had all finished eating, the older children

were shooed out into the street to play and little Johnny was put down for a nap. Mac accompanied Mr Jarrett and Tom Payne to visit the photographic studio near the Prefecture.

'Make yourself comfy. I'll get us a cuppa,' said Mrs Jarrett as she cleared the dishes and gestured towards the armchairs. I sat down and tried to think of something to say. There was something about her that made me feel tongue-tied.

'Thank you so much for that lovely soup. Do you have a servant or anyone who does the cooking? You must be so busy with the children as well as all the nursing work you do.'

'Well, I do most of the cooking myself. I've got Constanza, who helps out, but she is fairly unreliable and I swear we'd all starve or die of food poisoning if I trusted her with cooking unsupervised. You have to be careful with servants as they'll steal the hair off your head if you give 'em half a chance. Can't say I blame them, given what their poor little lives are like.'

'I'd be very grateful for some tips about cooking. I don't even know where to start.'

'Well the wood stove we had at first took a bit of getting used to but once I'd got the knack I was fine.'

'Actually, it's not just managing a stove,' I stuttered, and flushed with embarrassment. 'It's everything else. I've never cooked anything before. When I was a child we had servants and a cook; even when Papa died, we still had a housekeeper and at Doric Lodge someone else did the cooking.' I bit my lip in an effort to stop my tears welling up. I suddenly felt very stupid.

'Oh Lordy. I could tell you were classy and a bit of an innocent as soon as I clapped eyes on you.'

Her words stung but now I had started, I simply couldn't stop. 'There is so much to learn. I was really excited about coming here and ministering to these poor people. I've been preparing for this for years. But the truth is, I can't speak the language, I can't cook, I don't know the first thing about making a home or even how to be a proper wife...' I trailed off and my tears flowed. I felt ashamed and exposed. I'd blurted out too much. What would this woman think of me now? I wanted to run away and hide.

'Oh don't cry, dearie. You're just tired after the long journey and it's all new to you. No one's told you it was going to be easy. I had to learn just like you and there were no English women to help me when I first came.'

'I'm sorry. I'm just being silly. I'm sure it was much worse for you,' I dabbed my eyes. 'Please, don't tell my husband I was upset.'

'Don't be a silly goose. Now come on, dry your eyes. I'll leave Nellie in charge and we'll go and meet a woman who'll be a great help to you.'

Mrs Recharte opened the door to us and embraced Mrs Jarrett with a kiss on the cheek. She wore a simple grey woollen dress with mother of pearl buttons and lace trim. She held out her hand to me.

'You must be the new missionary nurse that your friend here has been eagerly awaiting. Welcome to our lovely city of Cuzco!' Although her accent was Spanish, her English was very good.

Her house was much larger than the Jarretts' and we

were led through the hallway to a small patio garden which was filled with shrubs and flowers. In one corner a pergola provided welcome shade. We sat and a servant girl brought glasses of lemonade.

'Mrs McNairn is going to need your help. I hope you can teach her as well as you did me when I first got here,' said Mrs Jarrett.

'It is lovely to meet you,' I said. I had recovered myself somewhat on the way to her house. 'I'm not completely useless. I can sew, sing, play the piano, bandage wounds, apply a poultice, cool a fever, calm a child and deliver babies. But I now realise that the missionary training school I attended forgot to teach us how to perform the practical tasks of real day-to-day living. And I'm afraid I only have a smattering of Spanish, since I didn't know I would be coming here until a couple of months ago.'

'Well, once you are settled, each day I will take you to the market to buy food and then I will show you how to cook it and we will speak only in Spanish,' said Mrs Recharte.

'That would be wonderful. Are you sure you have the time?' Once again, I felt tearful, but this time it was with relief.

'Mrs Recharte and I got to know each other when we started the bible reading evenings. She was one of our first converts,' said Mrs Jarrett proudly.

'Yes, it took me a while,' explained our hostess. 'I rejected the Catholic faith a long time ago when I was old enough to realize what those filthy priests get up to, and because I had read the excellent works of Darwin and Huxley, I found it hard to believe in any sort of divinity.

But now, I enjoy coming together with other like-minded people so that we can discuss the teachings of Jesus.'

We chatted for a while longer and took our leave, returning through the back streets to the Jarrett's house. I felt much better although I still imagined Mrs Jarrett thought I was far too "la-de-dah" to be much use in Cuzco. I was determined to prove her wrong. As we walked I pointed out a grubby, nearly naked four-year-old squatting over the gulley that ran down the centre of each street.

'It's the nippers that make your heart bleed, Mrs McNairn. They are everywhere, unwashed and uncared for. Some sleep in doorways or are crowded together in awful hovels. Many have to make it through their short little lives on their own. Just look at this little one picking maize grains out of the street drain to eat.'

'But where is her mother?' I asked.

'Well she might be working, or selling *chicha*, that's the local beer that everyone drinks. If this child was still a baby her mother would be carrying her tied onto her back. But she may even be away performing her *mita*. Every man and woman has to do unpaid service, called *mita* for a few months each year as part of the tax system. It dates back to the Inca times. They devised a system of work exchange so that rather than paying their taxes in the form of money each person spent a few months each year working for the state. This is how they were able to build their vast network of roads, terraces and temples. While the men were away their wives and families were provided for and so the system ensured that no one starved. But when the blooming Spaniards came they used the system to force the Indians to work in the mines or on the land for months on end while their families went hungry. Thousands died. And the system is still enforced today. Both men and women when they reach a certain age have to do their *mita,* and when that happens, sometimes an older child or an aunt will be left looking after the littl'uns. I've seen plenty of six or seven year olds made to be servants, working terrible long hours and getting beaten most days.'

Once we arrived back at the Jarrett house we made our farewells and returned to the hotel. I was excited to tell Mac about the plan to learn cookery and Spanish with the help of Mrs Recharte. Mac was equally excited to tell me about all the plans he had discussed with Mr Payne and Mr Jarrett about how he could begin his ministry. To start with, using his artistic training, he would help John Jarrett to improve the portrait photography business. Tom Payne would also teach him carpentry skills and there was a lecturer from the university who would gladly teach him Spanish and Quechua. Word would quickly spread that he had medical skills as few of the Indians could ever afford to pay a doctor.

'I'm sure it won't take me too long to master the basics of the language, and then I can start street preaching as well, just as I did before,' he said confidently. I wasn't so sure, but I didn't want to dampen his enthusiasm.

CHAPTER 5

Cuzco, Peru. 1904-5

We stayed at the hotel until after Christmas. At last we had acclimatised to the altitude and the stench of Cuzco. On Christmas morning, I gave Mac six hand-sewn white handkerchiefs embroidered with his initials, which I had secretly stitched on the voyage. He gave me a slim volume of Wordsworth's poems, which rather surprised me as I clearly remembered a conversation with him about how I disliked the poetry I had been made to recite as a child; but I was touched that he had also managed to conceal his gift on our long journey.

Instead of attending the cathedral service, all the missionaries came together in the meeting room with a dozen new converts. We sang carols while Mr Peters played a poorly tuned piano and Mac was flattered when they asked him to read the gospel story. I managed to exchange a few words in Spanish with a couple of the young converts from the university, who replied to me in impeccable English. It was all quite jolly. I was beginning to feel settled.

The rest of the Christmas Day we spent with Fred and Sadie Peters, the American missionaries who lived up the hill at San Elas. I had never met anyone from America before and immediately I felt a warm friendliness from them which I hadn't felt with the Jarretts.

'Oh, do call me Sadie. You English can be so formal at times!'

They had two delightful boys, Eric aged six and Cecil who was two, and within minutes of our arrival, I had Cecil sitting on my lap while I traced my finger around his tiny palm and recited "Round and round the garden" with him. He giggled with delight each time I tickled his armpits. The boys reminded me of my nephews and I felt a wave of homesickness. Sadie Peters was a good cook and the dish was not too spicy, although I did choke on my mouthful when Mr Peters told me that we were eating *cuy*, or roast guinea-pig.

Our plates were taken by away by a servant girl called Maria. Mrs Peters told us that when they had first set up house in Cuzco they'd needed a maid and Maria, aged eight, was sent to them. Her father was dead and her mother was cruel and had frequently beat her.

'You should have seen her when she first came. Her hair was all matted, crawling with lice. She had a ragged dress and no underclothes. We fed her, clothed her, taught her the alphabet and how to sew, clean the house and peel potatoes. She really thrived and loved being with us.'

'But after nine months,' Fred Peters continued, 'a businessman called *Señor* Marín came to our house and informed us that Maria now belonged to him. The child's mother was in prison for stealing and had somehow managed to persuade *Señor* Marín to pay the fine in exchange for her daughter who would become his slave and goodness knows what else. He dragged poor Maria from our house. Fortunately, although she was gone more than six weeks, we managed to convince a judge to return the child to us and the mother back to prison.'

'What an awful story,' said Mac as we watched Maria cleaning the plates. 'It must have been a relief when you were able to get her back.'

'I'm afraid this sort of thing is a common occurrence,' replied Mr Peters. 'If an Indian owes money for a fine or needs to pay the doctor for some medicine or the priest to bury a relative and he can't pay, his wife or his children will be taken away until he can find the money. Selling a child into slavery is sometimes their only solution and girls are often unwanted.'

As darkness fell we made our way back to the hotel; we were both quiet and thoughtful.

'It wasn't quite the Christmas I had imagined,' said Mac, 'but I think we shall do well here once we are settled and have a place of our own.'

'And maybe when we have a baby of our own,' I replied, giving him a shy smile.

'First things first, my dear.'

A few weeks later Mac found us a house of our own. It was in a little street close to the Church of Santa Domingo which had been built on Qoricancha, the site of the Inca Sun Temple. In Inca times this had been the most important place of worship; the courtyard had life-size llamas, corn stalks, flowers, birds and butterflies

– all made in solid gold. The walls had been covered in 700 sheets of gold studded with emeralds and turquoise, and the windows were constructed so that when the sun shone through them, worshipers would be almost blinded by the reflections off the precious metals. It was here that the mummified remains of the Inca leaders were kept on golden thrones. In that same room, there was a large gold disc which represented the sun, and on the opposite wall, a silver disc depicted the moon. But sadly, all the beauty was destroyed when Pizarro and his greedy *conquistadores* seized every scrap of gold and melted it down.

Unfortunately, the house that Mac found us rarely saw any sun. However, like many others, it was entered via a small sunny courtyard which was shared by several families. At least the main room had a small window and there were two bedrooms. With Tom Payne's help, Mac constructed a small table and two chairs and a friend of Sadie's found us a sturdy iron frame bed. We worked for the RBMU (Regions Beyond Missionary Union), and they had provided funds to enable us to set up house. Mac left me to furnish the house as I wished and I spent several happy mornings with Mrs Recharte haggling for blankets and rugs to introduce some colour into the otherwise dismal interior. Our trunk, now empty of the bibles we had brought with us, was covered with a cloth and doubled up as a wash stand and wardrobe. Mac whitewashed the walls of the main room and then had the ingenious idea of painting a mural of a garden scene with flowers and trees which covered the whole of one wall. I was so delighted when I first saw it finished. It was like having my very own garden.

Over the next few weeks, I tried to impress Mac with how determined I was to adapt to this new way of living. I kept reminding him that I could have ended up in the Congo where the facilities might have been even more primitive. The kitchen was tiny with just enough room for a wood stove and small sink with one tap. The Peruvians, I discovered, didn't go in for washing very much. It took me quite a while to cope with having to use the shared pail closet in the corner of the courtyard. I couldn't believe how primitive and unhygienic it was. But I was also desperately keen to impress Mrs Jarrett with my resilience and I forced myself to make jokes about the discomforts of Peruvian living.

At the end of each working day, just before dark, we joined the other missionaries in the meeting room above the cabinet making shop, for prayers and bible reading with the Indians and *Cholos* who worked there. Both English and Spanish were spoken and Mac was able to pick up essential Spanish phrases relatively easily. He also started lessons with a young man called Juan Rosaz, who, when he wasn't lecturing at the university, visited many of the Indian households and invited them to attend the bible reading classes.

Mac was very keen to start street preaching as soon as his Spanish was fluent enough, despite Payne and Jarrett warning him about the reaction he would attract from the local priests. They had both tried it in the early days but the fear of being seen by any of the clergy listening to the "Protestant heretics" as they were known, resulted in people passing by quickly, their faces averted. Instead, they suggested he find ways to advertise his medical expertise, since anyone could practice medicine as long as they didn't charge for it and this would be a much better way to win hearts and minds.

Mac thought it would be prudent to at least introduce ourselves to the local priest and so we attended a Sunday morning service at the Church of St Teresa where Father Carrillo was the priest in charge. The church was a long, high ceilinged hall with gaudy, gilt-framed oil paintings hung on either side of the walls. At the far end a huge golden altar was festooned with pink and red artificial flowers. Above this were statues of saints in yellow and purple robes adorned with strands of tinsel. The crowd which filled the church all knelt and the Indian women especially touched their foreheads to the ground and crossed themselves repeatedly. At intervals, a bell rang and a young priest waved the censor which belched pungent incense. In the background a harmonium played music, quite unrelated to whatever was occurring in the service, and at intervals small boys set off firecrackers by the front door. There were no actual hymns or prayers or sermons or readings. Worshippers came and went and the retinue of robed priests continued with the Mass, quite oblivious to it all. We were appalled.

At the end of the service Mac attempted to introduce himself to Father Carrillo; a stubby little man with a large nose, widely flaring nostrils and huge buck teeth. He looked Mac up and down, spat into a filthy handkerchief and muttered, 'Yet more of you heathen English to plague our streets.'

'Not at all,' stuttered Mac. 'I have medical skills. I am here to help.' But the priest had already turned away and disappeared through a small door.

Shortly after this encounter Mac was given his first opportunity to demonstrate these skills. One evening, Mrs Recharte, accompanied by a young girl, knocked on our door and requested his help.

'I apologise for disturbing you, Mr McNairn, but Angelina, my house girl, is in great distress. Apparently, her father has injured himself at work today but they cannot afford a doctor and I wondered if you might be able to help.'

'Of course, I'll come right away. Just let me fetch my medicine bag.'

'Shall I come with you?' I asked. They both nodded and Mrs Recharte said she would translate.'

The young girl led us up a maze of steep, narrow streets to the outskirts of the town. She walked so fast that we were quite breathless by the time we arrived at her father's house. Finally, we passed through two courtyards and entered a dark room. There was no window and the floor seemed alive with guinea pigs, scampering around. From what little light there was from the oil lamp, I noticed that the walls were covered in pictures of saints and angels. In one corner was a hen roosting on some sticks and in the other was a rough bedstead made from wooden boards placed together like a raft. On the bed lay a man in his late thirties, groaning and clutching his leg.

While we had been hurrying to the house, Mrs Recharte had warned Mac about what to expect. The Indians and *Mestizos* had many superstitious ideas about treating the sick. For sprains and fractures, they might kill a snake, cut it open and tie it around the injury and for bruises and wounds they often bound them with leaves or pieces of sheep's liver. Fortunately, Angelina's father had done neither. Mac was introduced to him by Mrs Recharte and, gesturing to the girl to bring the lamp closer, he knelt on the floor to examine the man's leg. Just below the knee was a large gash covered in matted blood and bits of straw. The straw had been used to staunch the flow of blood. While Mac was looking at the wound, Mrs Recharte had got the fire going and quickly boiled some water. Slowly Mac began to clean the wound.

'This is going to need some stitches. I think he might be better off at the hospital.'

'No hospital, no hospital,' cried the man.

'He is worried about the cost and that he might be told not to go back to his work,' explained Mrs Recharte.

'Well, I will attempt to stitch the wound myself but please tell him that it will hurt a great deal while I am doing it. If he rests the leg as much as he can and keeps the wound clean, it should heal alright.'

Once all this was explained, the man asked his daughter to fetch him some coca leaves and after he had chewed on them for a few moments, he signalled to Mac that he could begin stitching. Mac had heard about the anaesthetic properties of coca leaves, but had not yet seen anyone chew them. Mac couldn't help smiling as he opened his medical bag; this was the first time he had used it. Gently, using forceps, he pried away the pieces of straw and dirt from the wound and poured some antiseptic liquid over it. The man flinched but did not cry out. However, once the stitching began, the man yelled and squeezed his daughter's hand tightly until it was finished.

Just as we were about to leave, having done as good a

job as Mac could manage in the low light and filth of the house, Angelina gave him four hen's eggs wrapped in a tatty bit of cloth. 'No money, but please accept our gratitude,' she said as took his hand and shook it vigorously.

'Now you have performed your first medical task, word will quickly spread,' said Mrs Recharte as we walked back down the steep street to the centre of the town.

Mac was very proud of himself but when we were getting ready for bed he said. 'Oh goodness, Beatrice, what a wasted opportunity. I should have used the time to tell the poor man about the healing powers of Jesus.'

'Well I doubt very much that he would have heard you, given the pain he was in, but perhaps you could return in the next day or two to check that your instructions have been obeyed and you could try a little preaching then.'

I was quite pleased with my own successes. I had accompanied Mrs Jarrett on several visits to women who had recently been delivered of babies. A couple of days before this incident, Mrs Jarrett asked me if I would go on my own to visit a first-time mother, from the *gente decente* or upper-classes, who fortunately spoke good English. After I had said a few pleasantries to the mother and admired the baby, I asked for a basin of warm water so that I could show her how to give the baby his first bath. I was just about to put him in the water when the woman's sister stopped me. She had a cup in each hand. One cup contained alcohol and the other some greasy looking soup. She poured both cups into the water and stirred it around saying that this mixture would make the baby strong! I couldn't very well argue and they were all smiles when the baby splashed his hands in the water.

As the weeks passed I looked forward to spending the evenings with Mac. The room felt quite cosy once all the linseed oil lamps and tallow candles had been lit. I had learnt how to make some basic stews, despite the difficulties of cooking on the smoky wood stove. Over supper we would exchange stories about what we had seen or learnt during the day and sometimes we would practice our Spanish, though Mac was further ahead than me. Later, once I had washed all the plates and pots, we would sit in our armchairs and I would read to him from one of the Dickens novels I had brought with me. Reading about Victorian London made us both nostalgic and a little homesick.

Since we had both lost our mothers at an early age, neither of us had experienced "normal" family life with a mother and father spending their evenings together, but somehow this was just how we had imagined married life would be. Mac always worried that our house was so basic but I tried to reassure him by being very adaptable.

What still felt rather strange was what happened when it was time for bed. We had been married almost five months and at last we had a proper bedroom, but Mac still seemed to be uncomfortable about making love. Despite having older sisters, he knew nothing about a woman's monthly visitor or when was the best time to conceive a child. I wondered if he felt embarrassed that I seemed to know a little more than him about the mechanics of the sexual act and its consequences. During his training, he had concluded that sex should only be for procreation. But since he was adamant that we shouldn't have a child until we had been in Peru for at least a year, on the rare occasions we did have sex, he made sure that it was over as quickly as he could manage and he turned away from me at once, wracked with guilt. It wasn't at all what I had expected and unfortunately talking about it was impossible. I just waited and hoped it would get better.

Just before Easter, everyone began to talk about the annual procession through the streets in honour of *El Señor de los Temblores*. Tom Payne suggested that the best view was from the safe vantage point of a balcony on the Plaza de Armas and the Jarretts joined us there. Mrs Jarrett was keen to see what we would make of the ceremony. As the sun descended behind the mountains, the plaza began to fill with people. More and more arrived until there hardly seemed any space left and I was relieved that we were standing above them on the balcony. The atmosphere was strange. Unlike gatherings we had seen before, this crowd was hushed, as if a spell had been cast over them. Even though the light was fading the crowd was still full of colour. There were Indians in rainbow striped ponchos, wearing blue or silver hats; *Cholitas*, or working class girls in multi-coloured skirts and shawls; Cuzco aristocrats in black coats and young *señoritas* with black silk mantillas. The crowd waited silently, all eyes upon the closed cathedral doors. Eventually the huge doors opened and the strange apparition of the black crucified Christ, which we had seen in the cathedral on our first day emerged, carried by a dozen or more Indians. The figure was covered in the same gaudy flowers and the loin cloth glittered with gems. The procession slowly advanced across the Plaza, led by priests in rich robes and followed by a noisy brass band.

Clouds of incense rose from the swinging censors. As the litter approached most people knelt, while others were prostrate, their faces pressed in to the cobble stones.

'How strange and how powerful is the spell which the dead image of a Living Reality exercises over all these people,' remarked Mac to Mr Jarrett who was standing next to him.

'How right you are,' replied Jarrett. 'When I think of the devotion lavished upon this meaningless image by these people who have nothing, it makes me so angry. Just look at that withered old Indian down there. He will have walked for miles from his village just to be able to look at this spectacle. Look at the expression on his face, longing for something he doesn't really understand. He has come here to worship year after year, and yet he is still hungry, still ill-treated, still unsatisfied and soon he will die without ever knowing about the love of Christ. It's a sinful outrage.'

'And look, Mrs McNairn. Look at that young woman, barely a teenager, kneeling on the stones over there just on the outskirts of the crowd,' added Mrs Jarrett. 'See how she holds up her baby, with his chubby little hands in front of him, hoping that a blessing may reach him. It's so pitiful.'

I was struck by the contrast of the poor people desperate for some sort of miracle to relieve their suffering and the riches of the priests who maintained such power over them. It put any of my problems into perspective.

I was about to speak when the swaying black figure loomed towards us and then out of the plaza and into the surroundings streets. The crowd remained where they were.

Gradually the priests and the litter reappeared and it was inched back towards the cathedral. The crowd fell silent. Again, they waited. Then the statue paused and seemed to bow to each corner of the plaza, before it disappeared back into the gloom. Once the massive doors were shut a huge wail erupted from the crowd.

'They are wailing because they have seen their god for a brief hour and now they have to wait for another whole year,' said Payne.

'So, what happens now?' asked Mac.

'What happens now, my friend, is that instead of Cuzco being filled with rejoicing souls who have been fed and refreshed in spirit, they will all flock to another shrine, where in many *chicharias*, the fiery god alcohol is waiting to minister to them.'

CHAPTER 6

Cuzco. 1905

I had to hurry to keep up with the young girl as we passed the Church of San Francisco and Santa Clara to a little road which turned off from the Inca walls of the Calle Hospital. It was a route I knew well since many of the poor of Cuzco lived in this vicinity. But it was dark, the open drain had an awful stench, and I had to tread carefully to avoid tripping and falling into a mess of sewage. The girl had knocked on our door and begged me to come quickly to see her mother who had gone into premature labour and needed help. Her father was somewhere in the town, probably lying in a drunken stupor.

When we reached the house, I paused for breath, and looking around, I realised that one of the local white midwives lived upstairs. Why had she not been called? The girl pushed open the door and led me into a small room. In the corner was a woman who looked almost unconscious. I knelt down beside her, felt her brow which was cold and clammy and put my hand on her belly. There were faint contractions but when I lifted up the dirty sheet which covered her, I saw a large pool of blood. I asked the girl why she hadn't called on the midwife upstairs. 'We have no money to pay her. She won't come without money.' I was furious and strode to the stairway in the courtyard, hurried up the stairs and hammered on the nurse's door. 'Come down at once! There is a woman dying downstairs.' Despite the glow of a light under the door, no one answered.

I didn't know what to do. The woman would die without urgent medical attention. Perhaps I could run to the Calle Hospital and persuade someone to come out to this house. I sped back down the stairs and began to explain that I was going to summon help. But the girl was kneeling beside her mother, crying. It was too late. The woman was already dead.

Feeling quite numb, I said a short prayer, and with the daughter's help, found sufficient water to wash her poor mother and bundle up the bloodied bedclothes. The girl couldn't have been more than nine or ten. Now what? I couldn't leave her alone with the body of her mother and I wouldn't know where to start to look for the drunken father.

'What is your name?'

'Sophia.'

'Well, Sophia. I am going to take you back to my house and we will find your father tomorrow.'

Slowly we walked back through the now moon-lit streets to our own house. The poor child was exhausted. I made up a small bed with some of our extra blankets and waited beside her until she fell asleep. It was only then, when I had crept into bed beside my sleeping husband that I allowed myself to weep with the pity of it all.

The following morning Mac and I accompanied Sophia

back to her house where we found the father, now sober, sitting on a chair with his head in his hands. Mac explained what had happened and admonished him for neglecting his wife and daughter. When we turned to leave, young Sophia clung to me, imploring me not to leave. I gently removed her hands and promised I would visit her very soon.

On the way back to our house, I had an idea.

'Mac, do you think we could employ Sophia as our servant? As I am going to be the only English nurse for the next few months, I am going to be much too busy to manage the house and everything. And besides, we would be doing the father a favour if she is working for us and we can make sure she goes to school. Oh, do please say, yes.'

'If you think it might work, my dear, go ahead and ask her father, but just remember we cannot have every destitute child you come across working for us.'

Over the past few months my confidence had improved enormously. There had been many occasions when I had been able to demonstrate my competence in both nursing and midwifery and now I knew enough basic Spanish and Quechua to communicate sufficiently with those who sought my help. There was enough work for all of us to do and although Mrs Jarrett was nominally in charge and made most of the decisions, I had discovered that there were many things I could do on my own to gain the trust of the women, such as helping to sweep a room, or kiss a hurt finger, tie a baby's shoe or mend a schoolboy's broken slate. Such simple little things.

In the beginning, I had held Mrs Jarrett in awe. She seemed to be so capable, whether it was dressing a wound, teaching her children, or haggling in the market. But as the months passed, I realised that although superficially she appeared friendly, underneath there seemed to be strands of resentment. Mac too, had experienced some difficulties with John Jarrett, who constantly told him what was and wasn't possible and discouraged many of the new initiatives which Mac suggested. It was as if they both felt threatened by the energy and enthusiasm which we had brought with us. So, when the Jarretts announced that they were taking some leave in September and returning to England for a few months furlough, I felt both relieved and apprehensive about managing on my own. At the same time Sadie Peters, now pregnant with her third child, decided to return to America for the birth. This left me as the only English speaking woman in Cuzco and Tom Payne as the only other male missionary.

Once the Jarretts had left, Mac and Tom Payne worked well together. A number of university students were both eager to learn English and attend the bible study evenings which they now were able to hold without Jarrett's interference. Mac found that many of the more educated young men had long since abandoned the Catholic religion of their childhoods and knew all about the corruption of the priests. Unfortunately, their mothers and most women from the upper-classes still liked to appear to be devoutly Catholic. As Mr Payne had explained to us when we first arrived, church-going for women was more of a social than religious occasion. However, since the law stated that anyone in Peru could practice medicine as long as they took no fee, Mac's reputation as the *Medicinas Inglesas* had spread. He was welcomed into many high society houses by women who no longer trusted the local doctors.

At each visit, he would leave some pamphlets and explain his beliefs.

Juan Rosaz, the teacher from the university, who'd helped Mac learn Spanish, proved to be a most eloquent speaker. He had managed to persuade some of the Indians to attend meetings, even though at harvest time most were too busy. One evening we held our first meeting speaking only in Quechua. I looked around the room and noticed an elderly Indian man who stood up several times to ask questions. Looking at his heavily lined face, I tried to imagine him, not as an impoverished farm worker, but as man of influence and wealth at the court of Atahulpa. When Mac closed the meeting with a short prayer in his stumbling Quechua, the old man rose and repeated the prayer, word for word, with faultless pronunciation. I gave him such a big smile of encouragement and he bowed his head to me in acknowledgment.

Mac had numerous plans which he discussed at length with Tom Payne. Apart from the English classes for the university students, he was also keen to explore the villages in the hills and valleys around Cuzco and spread the Word to more Indians. We could both see that there was a need to teach basic hygiene to parents who had little concept of regularly washing either themselves or their children. I saw endless squalor in the poor families I visited. One fifteen-year-old girl, whose baby I had delivered, was living with an older woman in one tiny room. In all my nursing days, I had never seen anything to equal the dirt and vermin in that room. When I undressed the week-old baby it was covered in fleas and lice. I had to change all my clothes when I returned home and quickly plunge them into a pail of water.

The list of projects was endless. Mr Payne kept reminding Mac to slow down and take on one task at a time, but it was as though he was so determined, nothing anyone said could stop him from trying out yet another idea. I began to notice that whenever I told Mac of a successful visit I had made, he would tell me about something he had done or somewhere he had been. It seemed so silly. He didn't need to be competitive. There was quite enough work for us all. One evening, when Mr Payne had joined us for supper, Mac was called out to see a sick man. Tom Payne got up to leave as well.

'Oh, you don't have to go Mr Payne. Stay for a cup of tea and keep me company.'

'Yes, do stay. I'm sure I won't be long,' said Mac.

'Well thank you both. That was a most delicious supper.'

My cooking had definitely improved, and although everything I made was really just a variation of stew, I could if necessary muster up several different dishes, such as black potato soup or pumpkin fritters. Mac's favourite was *tamales*, corn dumplings filled with ground pork. I cleared the table, made the tea and gestured to Mr Payne to sit in an armchair.

'Mac is very keen, isn't he? I do wish he'd slow down a bit. I am quite worried that he'll wear himself out if he keeps going like this,' I said.

'Believe me, Mrs McNairn, I have told him over and over again to take his time. It's not a race, not a competition for who can make the most converts. Rome wasn't built in a day and all that. I really admire him but he doesn't have your gentleness and sometimes his passion can be mistaken for arrogance. He's a real stubborn Scot, isn't he?'

He looked at me intently and smiled. I blushed. I felt a mixture of confusion and relief; confused by his comments about my gentleness and relieved that he understood my perspective. I busied myself and poured more tea and he spoke of his plans to gather sufficient funds to buy a plot of land to start a mission farm which would employ many Indians as well as providing an opportunity to teach them the bible, away from the prying noses of the priests. I began to relax again and soon found myself asking,

'Can I ask you a personal question, Mr Payne?'

'Well that depends on how personal,' he replied with that same inquisitive smile.

'Why is someone as kind and pleasant as yourself not married?' There, I had blurted it out, and when he looked a bit taken aback, I chided myself for being so intrusive.

'Well it's a long story. I'm sure you don't want to hear it all.'

'I apologise, Mr Payne, if I have been inappropriate. I have no right to ask, but you will find me a good listener.'

'Well, there was a girl once. She was called Lily. We spent a lot of time together while we were growing up, when she lived next door to my family. We were best friends.'

He paused, as if he was considering what to say next. 'I have only ever longed for two things in my life. First was to marry Lily and second was to do something that would make a real difference to the world. But sadly, when we told her parents of our plans, to our complete surprise, they absolutely forbade it. Her family are devout Catholics and I was brought up as a Protestant. They told us that we were both far too young and since I didn't seem to have any financial security, our marriage was out of the question. I pleaded with them that I would wait for her and that I would get myself a good job. But within weeks, they had packed her off to a finishing school in Switzerland and one year later, more or less forced her to marry some dimwit called Murphy, a wealthy banker almost twice her age. I was broken hearted and reckoned that the only way I could survive it was to disappear halfway round the world. There you have it Mrs McNairn. That's my sad story.'

He blew his nose on a large white handkerchief. 'I think after this confession you could probably call me "Tom" when it's just us.'

'I'm so sorry. It must have been awfully hard for you coming out here all alone – Tom.'

'Well, as long as you can keep a secret, I haven't given up all hope. Just last week I received a letter from her. Apparently, a couple of months ago her husband was killed in a riding accident. Although she is still in the mourning period, reading between-the-lines, I think she would like us to re-establish contact. Perhaps now we are both a bit older, she won't give a fig what her parents have to say.'

'So, do you think you will be able to bring her out here?'

'Steady on! You're just as impatient as that husband of yours.'

At that moment, Mac walked back in and without thinking I told him Tom's news. 'Well done, old man, I can't recommend marriage highly enough,' Mac said, planting a kiss on my head.

'So much for my little secret, Mrs McNairn. But please, not a word to anyone else. I don't want to go counting my chickens.'

Sophia coming to work for us was a great success. She had clearly been doing similar chores for her parents, so I no longer had to worry about doing our laundry, cleaning the pots or peeling potatoes. I was just fluent enough in both languages and so I took Sophia with me to the market to buy food and I also made sure that she went to school each day. I introduced her to Mrs Recharte and to some of the other ladies with whom I visited regularly, and seeing how warmly they greeted the young girl, I longed to have a daughter of my own.

In the middle of December, it seemed as if my wish was going to come true. Even though I knew it was very early days, I broke my good news to Mac.

'Are you absolutely sure?' he asked, frowning. 'I thought we had been very careful and besides, we agreed we would wait until we were properly settled.'

'But we will have been here nearly eighteen months by the time its due.'

'But Beatrice,' he replied irritably. 'There is so much work for both of us to do and I'm not sure I am ready for babies.'

I was shocked and upset. Why wasn't he as happy as I? I turned away from him to hide the tears in my eyes. Mac went to put on his coat and hat. He hesitated and then came back to where I stood. 'I'm sorry Beatrice. It is wonderful news. I just wasn't expecting it quite yet.' He put his hand tentatively on my shoulder, but I shrugged it off and busied myself with the stove. He tried to make it right for me throughout the evening, but he couldn't take back what he'd said, and for the first time in our married life, we went to bed on a quarrel.

But two weeks later I suffered a miscarriage. Mac was out on a visit and didn't see me doubled up with pain. When he did return, he was alarmed to find me lying on our bed with my face to the wall. I had been crying on and off for a few hours after I'd dealt with all the rags and mess. He sat on the bed beside me, stroked my hair, and kept saying how sorry he was. He seemed so worried that somehow he had caused the miscarriage with his reaction to my pregnancy, that in the end it was me comforting him. I had to explain to him that it was common to lose a first baby, especially in the first trimester and that it shouldn't affect my health or future pregnancies.

After a couple of day's rest, I went back to my normal duties and I could see how relieved he was. I tried to hide how I was feeling inside. What if I would never be able to hold on to a pregnancy? I had come across plenty of women who'd had repeated miscarriages as well as delivering my fair share of stillbirths. Part of me wanted to try and become pregnant as soon as possible so that I could reassure myself. Despite Mac telling me that he'd regretted being so rigid about when we should have a child, I didn't want to risk his annoyance if I tried again too soon. I felt so lonely and wished my sister Susannah was nearby instead of thousands of miles away in England. She would have understood.

CHAPTER 7

Cuzco. 1906

The Jarretts returned to Cuzco in the New Year. I got myself in a bit of a stew as I imagined that they would disapprove of how we had managed things in their absence. But to my surprise the three-month furlough in England had done them a lot of good. They were well rested and John Jarrett was delighted with how hard Mac and Tom had worked during their absence, especially with the bible study meetings which were now quite well attended. Even Mrs Jarrett was quite complimentary when I told her about some of the tricky births I'd had to cope with. I realised that we would never be close, but perhaps now we could become slightly better friends. The children had all grown and were more boisterous than ever, especially little Johnny who had just turned four. And when the Peters returned from America a couple of weeks later with their two older boys and four-month-old baby son, Leighton, it seemed as if there were children everywhere. I found it so hard to conceal my envy, but I told neither of the women about my miscarriage. Stupidly I felt ashamed; as if I had failed somehow and I didn't think they'd understand.

With the turning of the year, though we never discussed it, somehow Mac and I resolved to leave our difficulties behind us. Surviving our first major quarrel had somehow strengthened our relationship.

Over the time I had been in Cuzco, I had grown to love the city; such a strange mix of Inca and Spanish. In some parts the different styles of architecture seemed to shout at each other, but in a few areas, both blended well. In the daytime it was always full of light, colour and bustle – such a contrast to the dismal greyness of London. It was never too cold or too hot. Most days it was sunny with pale blue skies, although in the early months of the year rain showers were quite common. One evening, after a particularly showery day, we took a stroll after our evening meal. The rain had washed the streets clean of the usual dirt and sewage and the cobbles glistened in the lamplight. The air felt fresh although it was a little chilly since the sun had long since set and I was grateful for the pale grey alpaca shawl that Mac had given me for Christmas. It was made from baby alpaca wool; wool which is taken from the underside of the neck of a one year old animal and it is far warmer and silkier than sheep's wool. I loved it.

There was hardly anyone about. Passing through one of the narrow streets, I stopped and ran my hand over the giant boulders and along the faint lines where they joined.

'How these stones were put in place never ceases to amaze me,' I said. 'Just think of what intriguing tales they could tell us.'

'I've come to think of Cuzco as such a sad place,' Mac replied. 'It's like a graveyard of buried hopes and possibilities. Sometimes I can almost sense the ghosts of those old warriors, both Indians and Spanish, who loved and fought and died in those dark days. It's as if they still haunt the streets.'

'What do you mean?' I asked, taking his hand as we emerged into the plaza.

'I feel it most on those nights when the full moon hangs over Sacsayhuamán and casts weird shadows in the narrow streets. It's then that I get glimpses of those restless ghosts of the past. They lurk in the shadows of those magnificent heraldic beasts which are carved on the doorways. And whenever I walk under these pillared arches I can hear the echo of their footsteps as if they are marching off to battle with their clanking armour. Listen. Can you hear it?' He paused and listened.

'I'm not sure,' I said. I felt something but it could have just been the wind. Something certainly felt rather ghostly. I shivered. 'It's time we were getting back.' We retraced our steps but once again Mac stopped by the Inca wall. This time he put his ear against the stone.

'It's here,' he whispered, pulling me towards him. 'Here in these old Inca streets are the ghosts I love best; sad ghosts, soft treading, with no clank of sword or clink of mail – dark wistful eyes, a glint of gold, a gleam of colour, pale in the moonlight; and sometimes a sound of sobbing, a moisture that might be tears.'

I had never heard him speak so eloquently – such a change from his usual preachiness. I kissed his cheek and as we walked back to the house I smiled to myself with a quiet contentment. I am convinced that it was on this night in early April that little Margaret was conceived. I kept my pregnancy a secret from everyone. This time, I had to be absolutely sure.

June came, and with it, yet another festival. Inti Raymi was an Inca ceremony held during the winter solstice with the aim of coaxing the sun to return after the longest night. (In the southern hemisphere, the winter solstice falls in June, not December.) When the Spanish conquered Peru, the Inca ceremony conveniently coincided with the Catholic feast day of John the Baptist and for many years the two had been combined. Peruvians love any excuse for feasting and getting dreadfully drunk, and with a typical muddling of teachings from Rome, John the Baptist became their patron saint of butchers. When I enquired how this was so, the simple answer was that St John he had said "Behold the Lamb of God!"

On the eve of the fiesta, wooden frames adorned with flags and loaded with fireworks were erected in the plaza. Several huge bonfires were also built on a platform outside the cathedral. From the green ridge of the fortress of Sacsayhuamán flags waved and all night long I could hear the sound of trumpets. On the day of the festival we made our way to the plaza where both Indian men and women were leading sheep, lambs and even llamas actually into the cathedral. There, they gathered around an image of John the Baptist with a silver lamb in his arms. At the side of nearly every woman was a sheep, nibbling bread from their hands, bleating softly, or being led forward for a blessing. They were all decorated with bright rags of cloth, their wool being tied up with a hundred little coloured bows. I was sad to see the men; big, dirty, awkward men, with dusty sandals and tangled masses of black hair, kneeling in silent adoration, some even had tears streaming down their cheeks. The church and priest with all the ceremonies, ornaments and trappings were what they worshiped. They knew nothing of the real God.

We left the cathedral just as the fireworks began to rip through the air. The noise was deafening but it was a wonderful sight. I had loved fireworks all my life and could never resist joining in with the "oohs" and "ahs" of the crowd. Later we followed the litter bearing the image of the Inti, dressed in tin foil and glittering gold, as it made its way up to Sacsayhuamán, where more fireworks erupted as darkness fell. Then the huge bonfire was lit and a llama was "sacrificed" to the Sun. After a while we walked back to our house knowing that drinking and dancing would continue all night.

'What an amazing spectacle!' I said. 'I do so love watching fireworks. It reminds me of bonfire night when I was a child and Papa used to take us to the common.'

'Fireworks are all very well, but just imagine how much alcohol will be consumed all night,' muttered Mac.

'Yes, but who can blame a poor Indian for enjoying a day of feasting and drinking, which for once, is encouraged by the Church?' I asked.

'Oh, it suits the priests well enough who encourage their mindless idolatry. But with their minds thus dulled and debauched how can they ever receive or retain the good news which we are trying so hard to impress upon them? Our only hope for the future lies with their children whom we must try and save from these appalling vices.'

'Oh Mac, don't be cross. I know you're right, but it all takes time and you are always too impatient.'

He made no reply and I felt my excitement fizzle away like air escaping from a balloon.

Since the return of my fellow midwives our work had steadily increased as more women sought our help and attended our meetings. Sadie still had six-month-old Leighton to look after and so she often took the night calls when her husband, Fred, was available to look after the children. Mrs Jarrett's children were now attending a proper school as she had no time to teach them at home and young Johnny was often left in the care of Luciana who had replaced Constanza as their house girl. Johnny was an adorable child but he was quite a handful with his tremendous energy and a will of his own.

One morning I called at the Jarrett's house to collect a new supply of lint and bandages which had arrived from England. I knew that Mr Jarrett had gone to Arequipa and was not due back for a few days. When I arrived the three older children were playing a card game around the table. 'No school today?' I asked. 'Where is your mother?'

Nellie pointed to the staircase. Upstairs I found Mrs Jarrett sitting beside Johnny's bed, holding a cloth to his fevered brow. She glanced up at me with tired eyes.

'He's been poorly for a few days now,' she said and turned back to the child. His little face was flushed and he cried as if he was in pain.

'He's had all the usual coughs and colds but this one seems a bit worse. I can't leave him for a moment and I haven't had time to get those littl'uns off to school. Luciana should be here but she's quite useless,' she said briskly.

'Don't worry Mrs Jarrett, I'll sort the children out. Johnny needs you. But give it a few days and I'm sure he'll be much better.' I collected the medical supplies I needed, got the children dressed and led them down the road to the school.

Early the following morning I was surprised to see Luciana on our doorstep. She looked terrified and begged me to come quickly. When I got to the Jarrett's house the other children were huddled round the table, still in their night clothes and Kathy was crying. I never expected what awaited me upstairs. Johnny still had a high fever and he'd had terrible diarrhoea throughout the night. Mrs Jarrett held him on her lap, rocking him back and forth. Her face was ashen, exhausted.

'What is it? How is he?' She didn't seem to hear me. I knelt down beside the two of them and felt the fever in the child's brow. She gently lifted up his little vest and I saw the tell-tale pink spots all over his chest and tummy. It was typhoid. I touched her hand. 'I am so very sorry. Have you any idea how...' I trailed off, thinking this was not the time for questions.

'I don't have eyes in the back of my head,' she snapped. 'I can't watch him all the time, along with everything else.'

'Of course not. I wasn't suggesting anything. This isn't your fault.'

'I told Luciana over and over again to not let him touch anything in the street,' she continued as if I hadn't spoken. 'But last week I saw for myself. Johnny was with a couple of other kids poking about in that filthy, stinking gulley with his fingers while the silly girl was too busy chatting with her friends.'

She began to cry. I put my arm round her shoulder for a moment and went back downstairs.

'Luciana, please go quickly and fetch Mr McNairn. You should find him at the carpentry shop near the plaza.' She scuttled out the door. 'Now Nellie, I want you to be a very good girl, get Harry and Kathy dressed and take them to Auntie Sadie's house and stay there. You know where that is, don't you?' She nodded.

Then I boiled some water, took some to make tea, and poured the remainder into a basin to take upstairs, so that we could give the child a wash and clean him up. I knew I had to be very careful to limit the risk of his infection spreading either to myself, or the others. Mrs Jarrett was too exhausted to refuse and she allowed me to take Johnny from her arms, wash him, put clean clothes on him and lay him back under the covers. He was floppy in my arms and whimpered in pain. Mrs Jarrett stroked his head and once he'd fallen asleep she was able to drink some tea. She looked haggard from lack of sleep and quite bewildered. Mac arrived and confirmed what we both knew was the truth. Between us we stayed with her all day making sure that she had some sleep herself.

Mr Jarrett was on his way back from Arequipa and so there was no way to warn him. When he finally arrived the following day, it was too late.

Johnny's death shocked us all. Sadie Peters kept the older children at her house for a few days while Fred and Mac tried to negotiate with the authorities for the child to be buried in sacred ground. But the priests refused, insisting that only Catholics could be buried in the local cemetery. Eventually Mac secured permission for him to be buried in the same small plot up the hill on the outskirts of the town where Will Newell had been buried.

For several days, Mrs Jarrett refused to eat or talk or do anything. She barely slept and either lay on Johnny's bed clutching one of his teddy bears or sat in the armchair staring at the wall. Her husband wandered around in a daze. Since Luciana had been sacked, I almost lived there for a while, cooking meals for them all and eventually I coaxed her into having some soup. It was only when Nellie, Harry and Kathy returned from staying with Sadie and she saw their distraught little faces that she was able to rally herself to take care of them.

CHAPTER 8

Cuzco. 1906

Not long after Johnny's death, when life had sort of returned to normal, Tom Payne returned to England for his first leave in several years. I was sad to see him go; he was so easy to be with and he had become a good friend to both of us. We knew he was going back to see how things were with Lily and I hoped he would return to us as a married man. Together we waved him off.

'I think my dear Mac,' I started nervously, 'that the next time we see him, I shall be holding our own baby in my arms.' I had agonised for over a week about how best to break the news and I knew that I couldn't conceal my bump for much longer.

'Are you sure?'

'Well I am about thirteen weeks gone so, yes, I am absolutely sure. The baby should be born in mid-December.'

He turned and drew me towards him, 'That is wonderful news, Beatrice, but you should have told me before. You have been working far too hard for a woman in your condition, you should be resting surely.'

'Don't be such a silly,' I laughed, so relieved by his reaction. 'After last time, I had to be sure. I am fine and like every other working woman I am quite able to continue as normal for many months yet.'

'Do the others know?'

'No, I don't know how to tell Mrs Jarrett. How can I celebrate being pregnant when she has just lost her child?'

'Oh, come now Beatrice. Surely she wouldn't begrudge you this, and besides she does have her other three children.'

'Having other children never makes up for the one that you have lost,' I replied, rather too sharply. 'Don't ever think that.' He looked a bit taken aback.

'How about if I speak to John Jarrett first so that he can break the news to her, and you can tell Fred and Sadie.'

At last I could share my excitement and my anxieties. Everyone was pleased for us and even Mrs Jarrett joked with me that now I would experience for myself what childbirth was really like.

Mac and Fred Peters had planned to start visiting some of the outlying villages which lay about a day's ride from Cuzco. Once Mac knew about my condition, he was reluctant to leave me, but he was eventually persuaded that I would manage perfectly well without him. I didn't tell him, but I rather relished the thought of having the house to myself.

Their mission to the villages was of mixed success. Mac decided he wouldn't take any medical supplies with him; he wanted to rely on the power of his preaching and the pamphlets which he and Fred had carefully printed in both Quechua and Spanish. Setting off with a couple of borrowed mules they followed the old tracks which wound up into the steep mountains and down again into fertile valleys. For many miles, they saw no one. Most Indians cultivated the land but they did not own it. Usually they were allowed a small portion for themselves in return for their labour. Many still cultivated the terraces that their Inca ancestors once farmed. These terraces needed careful irrigation to produce crops and were often so precipitous that one wrong move of the plough would send the farmer toppling fifty feet down into the valley below.

On the first day they stopped at a small, thatched shepherd's hut by a stream and called out a greeting in Quechua. A woman emerged from the dark doorway and stared at them. Then her husband appeared and offered them some *chicha* beer. They refused the beer, showing that they had water bottles and asked if they could be filled up. They were also offered some milk which they drank gratefully. Two small children appeared from the hut dressed in knitted caps with woollen cloths tied round their bodies. Although his Quechua was still rather basic, Mac told the family the story about the feeding of the five thousand and when they smiled and asked a few questions, he was convinced that this was where some of their mission work lay, not solely in the centre of Cuzco, but also in the mountains and valleys amongst these innocent and uneducated Indians.

They rode further on and came to a small village where they planned to stay in the village inn.

'The innkeeper gave us some soup and showed us a couple of mats in the corner where we could sleep,' Mac told me as we sat together on the evening he returned. 'Fred was snoring within minutes, but I felt quite wound up and I couldn't sleep. I opened the door, as quietly as I could and stepped out into the cool air. Beatrice, I don't think I can convey the half of what I saw. Around me were the dark silhouettes of the mountains and in the velvety darkness above, hung a blossom of stars. For once there was no breeze and apart from the distant sound of rushing water far down in the valley there was a profound stillness all around. I wish you had been there too because I felt quite overwhelmed by the beauty of it and at the same time so humbled that God chose me to come here to minister to these people.'

He fell silent and I could see part of him was still out there amongst the stars.

'So what happened the next day, Mac, to make you so dispirited?'

'Well, the following day we wandered around the village distributing our pamphlets and when anyone took the slightest interest, I spoke to them about the love of Christ. We thought it was all going so well, especially when some of them looked genuinely grateful, even though they held the pamphlets upside-down, since none of them could read. However, that evening, the innkeeper warned us that the village priest was furious and had seized as many pamphlets as he could grab and torn them up in a fury, scattering the pieces over the cobbles. I couldn't believe it, so we went outside to see for ourselves and found a small crowd of villagers, led by the priest, approaching. They were shouting and waving their fists at us. I felt so angry since I recognised several of the women who'd been only too grateful to hear what I'd said that morning. It's those damn priests. Everyone is too scared of their power.'

'Oh my goodness, how frightening,' I said.

'Naturally we were alarmed and had to retreat back inside. The innkeeper said we should leave immediately but we managed to persuade him to let us stay for a few hours while the crowd dispersed. So in the half-light of dawn we saddled the mules and headed out of the village on what we thought was the narrow track we had arrived on. Despite the early hour there were several people up and about who witnessed our departure and we tried not to make any eye contact. But after a short while, we heard running footsteps and a man was shouting behind us. Convinced he was about to attack we urged the mules to go faster. But here is where God works in mysterious ways Beatrice. The man dashed up beside me, grabbed the bridle of my mule and told me breathlessly that we were going the wrong way. This route would take us high into the mountains and the path was completely blocked by a landslide! I can't tell you how foolish and relieved we felt as we turned the mules around and headed in the correct direction, back towards Cuzco.'

'Thankfully, you are safe home now. Perhaps it wasn't such a good idea.'

'I am a little discouraged, my dear, but next time I shall take my medical bag with me. If I want to spread the Word, I must find a way to get past the power of the priests. And if I can show God's love through my medical bag, then that is how I shall do it. But I think I'll wait until Tom returns and make some trips with him.'

Earlier in the year John Jarrett had written to the Missionary Society to ask if they could possibly send us another nurse. He didn't expect an immediate response but in September, fresh from their training, Miss Pinn and Miss Wahnrow arrived. Ethel Pinn was a tall woman with an abundance of energy and humour. Edith Wahnrow was the exact opposite; short, plump, quiet and very serious. They had become the best of friends while they were completing their nurse training at St Thomas' Hospital, and what's more, they both already spoke a smattering of Spanish quite fluently. It was certainly good to have more help as I was becoming nicely fat with my baby growing inside me. I loved feeling her kick and wriggle, even if she did disturb my sleep.

A suitable property was found near to the Jarretts' house where we set up a small clinic where the two new nurses would be based. They had brought plenty of medical supplies with them and once word got round, there was always a queue of people waiting to be helped. I was amazed how quickly the women settled in. At last I was no longer the newcomer and I enjoyed showing them the town and taking them on home visits.

Scarcely a day passed without one of us being called to visit a poor home. Usually it was the children. So many parents seemed devoid of the most elementary ideas of how to care for children and child deaths were common. Quite often a woman would bring us a child suffering from diarrhoea or even dysentery. Upon asking what she fed the child, her reply might be "Oh anything, meat, *chocolo* (Indian corn), coffee, anything." Sometimes the child was only a few months old. It was a wonder that they survived at all, and sadly girl children had hardly any value at all. But teaching them hygiene and child care was a powerful factor in winning the hearts that might otherwise be closed against us.

When Tom did return, it was surprises all round. I was eight months pregnant and he arrived with Lily as his wife. She had indeed defied her parent's wishes and married the man whom she had always loved. I liked her immediately. She looked so young, indeed she was only twenty-four, and she had lovely fair hair and the most sparkling pair of blue eyes I'd ever seen. But looking at the nice clothes she wore as compared with my ancient skirt and patched blouse, I did worry about how she would cope with the level of poverty all of us had become so used to. I understood how Mrs Jarrett probably felt when she saw me for the first time. But seeing how happy Tom was to have finally won his sweetheart helped me put those worries aside. Together he and Lily were going to put into practice the plans to establish a missionary farm which would offer both jobs and housing for many Indians. I hoped it wouldn't be too far away from Cuzco.

Suddenly it seemed that our little community of English speaking missionaries had doubled in size. The schools and university were open and so the city was full of young men who came from the provinces to attend classes. Many of them found their way to our meetings and Mac was very keen to start English classes for them. *Señor* Juan Rosaz, the university lecturer who had helped Mac learn Spanish, was eager to help.

I had calculated that our baby would arrive in the middle of December but the date came and went and I found it increasingly hard to get around with my belly being so large. When my ankles became a bit swollen, Flo, (as I was now allowed to address Mrs Jarrett), ordered me to rest. It had taken a while but eventually Flo had thanked me for the help I had given her with Johnny. Now that we were on first name terms, she called me "Beat" or "Beatie". She had appointed herself as my midwife and although I was nervous I was grateful for her expertise. However, with little to do except sew yet more baby clothes, my mind kept turning to my mother and my sister, Lilian, both of whom had died of a haemorrhage while giving birth. I had witnessed enough deaths to know that if anything like that happened to me, I too would be unlikely to survive.

But with it being our third Christmas in Cuzco, I tried to remain cheerful and hide my worries. With Lily's willing help, I was able to make a few gifts for Miss Pinn and Miss Wahnrow.

The pains started on the day after Boxing Day. Mac wanted to send for Flo immediately, but I knew it would be a while before I would need her. He paced the room asking every few minutes if I was all right.

'Oh, for goodness sake, Mac, go and fetch Flo and ask John if he'll take you out for a walk. I can't have you pacing up and down like this or I'll go mad.'

'But I can't leave you. What if the baby comes while I am gone?'

'Dearest, nothing is going to happen for quite a while. Now just go!'

Flo came and I couldn't have had a better companion; at last I felt accepted by her. I learnt much about her early days in Cuzco and how John had narrowly escaped being attacked. She told me all about her own children's birth and helped me to breathe through the pain. She had been right when she'd told me that no one can really understand what it is like until they have experienced it for themselves. In those few hours, I learnt more about helping someone bring a precious baby into the world than I had ever learnt at Doric Lodge.

In the early hours of December 27th my little baby girl was born. I wrapped her up in the soft grey alpaca shawl Mac had given me the previous year. We named her Margaret Bellamy. Margaret, or rather "Peggy", was the name of my very first nanny, whom I adored. Bellamy was my mother's family name. And like all mothers, I thought that Peggy was the most beautiful baby I had ever seen.

CHAPTER 9

Cuzco. 1907

Those first few months after Peggy was born were very challenging. I had assumed that motherhood would come to me naturally, given all the babies I had tended. But having my own was different; I was so anxious about doing it right, terrified in case she caught an infection, and reluctant to leave her with anyone else. Both Sadie and Flo warned me how tired I would become if I tried to manage everything and they were right.

Eventually one afternoon, I was persuaded to leave Peggy with Sadie for a few hours. Mac wanted us to walk up to Sacsayhuamán; the old Inca fortress and religious complex which towered over Cuzco. The climb took us quite a while and I realised how unfit I had become. I had only been up there once since we had been in Cuzco and I had forgotten its grandeur. Three massive, zig-zagging walls, stacked one upon another like terraces, had once protected the fortress from attackers. Each wall was built of colossal boulders, the tallest of which was at least thirty feet high. It was wonderful to look down upon our lovely city; a jumble of pink and red roofs, broken by squares and plazas of grey and brown. The green hills before us were mottled with sunshine and shadow and we sat and watched the sun setting.

'I have so missed just being with you, my dear,' said Mac as he took my hand. 'I mean, I do love the baby, but she seems to take all your attention and we hardly have any time to ourselves these days.'

I couldn't believe he was actually jealous of a baby, but perhaps I had rather neglected him. 'I'm sorry Mac. The others told me how time consuming babies could be but I hadn't realised that you minded.'

'Well perhaps after today, we could do this sort of thing a bit more often and we do need you back at the prayer meetings. Why can't you leave Peggy with Sophia?'

'Don't be ridiculous, Mac. Sophia is only twelve years old. I couldn't possibly think of leaving her in charge of our baby,' I replied. He looked hurt and pulled his hand away. I hadn't meant to sound so cross, and as usual, I had to coax him to feel better before he went into one of his sulks.

'No, Mac, you are right. I have been very wrapped up in Peggy's welfare and I will return to my duties very soon. I'll get some help from either Flo or Sadie when they aren't too busy, and I suppose I could find a proper nurse for her.'

'Thank you my dear. Let's not quarrel. This evening is far too beautiful.' He pointed to the horizon. The sun had gone but the snow-topped mountains still caught the pink of its glow. 'Let us pray that the light, which the Indians lost because of the evil of Rome, will shine in their lives once more.'

We walked back down to the city as the first stars began

to peep through and the bells of the cathedral began to ring for the evening mass.

I resumed many of the activities I had been doing before, and whenever I could, I took Peggy along with me. I was still feeding her myself and so I could never be away from the house for too long. I kept being asked when she was to be baptised and I had to explain that she would only be baptised when she was old enough to accept the love of Christ into her heart. Whenever I said this, women looked very grave and crossed themselves.

When she was only about four months old we had important visitors. Mr Harry Gratton Guinness came to stay in Cuzco with his daughter Geraldine. He was the eldest son of our founder, Dr Henry Gratton Guinness, who, at eighty no longer travelled. Geraldine was nearly nineteen and was already a well-travelled girl. She announced that she was planning to write a history of Peru and its people and wanted to visit everywhere to learn about the Peruvian way of life. Her father was travelling the length and breadth of South America to visit all the missionary settlements of the RBMU (Regions Beyond Missionary Union) and he stayed only a short while, leaving Geraldine in our care. She was a delight and her enthusiasm was infectious. She adored Peggy and was a great help, playing with her while I had household chores or mission work to do. She paid visits with each of us to tend to our patients and her singing at prayer meetings drew quite a following.

One afternoon we paid a visit to Maria, a girl from a middle-class family. In the two storey house the floor was made of bricks and the walls of mud which were decorated with paper figures cut out from fashion-books, advertisements and visiting cards. A dirty curtain partially veiled the entrance to the bedroom where piles of clothes were strewn over the floor. The furniture consisted of a rickety couch, a chair, a trunk, and several fragments of packing cases. Her mother offered us some *chicha* beer which we declined and I greeted Maria's younger siblings who were playing a noisy game in the corner. Maria was a pretty girl of sixteen and she had a baby girl of three months old called Marcela. (No one talked about who the father had been.) When we arrived, Maria was stuffing large chunks of an orange (both flesh and peel) into Marcela's mouth. Geraldine hadn't believed me when I'd told her about what babies were fed. I expressed my concern but Maria told us proudly, 'Oh the baby is very good, she eats anything.'

It was a strange picture; this childish young mother, her dirty baby taken straight from the bed where she had slept in yesterday's frock, being fed all sorts of unsuitable foods, with the family around her, gnawing oranges and spitting the pips onto the floor. No wonder so many children in Peru died before they even reached their fifth birthday.

I reminded them all again about the bible study evenings and the English classes.

'Oh, I would love young Luis to learn English,' said the mother. 'To do well in Arequipa or Lima one must have good English, but his reading is very slow.'

'So why did Luis and his brother not come to the meeting last week, I was expecting him?' I asked.

'Poor Luis, he had a boil on his bottom and he could not sit down.' The sister laughed and Luis flushed red. 'Don't laugh, Manuela, it was very sore. He and Manuela will certainly be there next week.'

'Can we sing that lovely song we sang last time?' asked Manuela.

'You mean "*Dolor y muerto sufriendo, al hombre vida dió*"?' I replied, 'Suffering sorrow and death, He gave life to man.'

'Yes, that one. It has a lovely tune and your friend Señora Geraldine sang it so nicely.'

We chatted about many other things and after we left, I said to Geraldine,

'I know that Luis and his sisters won't come to the prayer meeting. They always agree when I visit them but they are all too frightened in case the priest finds out and punishes them.'

'Doesn't that make you feel frustrated?' asked Geraldine.

'Well, yes and no. I hope that our Christian charity rubs off on them and that given time they will see how much happiness and love can be found through believing the message we bring. The more the priests rant and rave the louder we sing with a smile on our faces and love in our eyes.'

While I had been introducing Geraldine to our work in Cuzco, I had really missed Tom and Lily. They had been away for a few weeks exploring the *Puna* – or hills about twenty miles from Cuzco – and had found an excellent site at Urco for the new farm. With money from the Missionary Society, their aim was to provide Indian families with a decent place to live and in return they would all work together to grow crops and tend livestock. Their families and children would be taught English and everyone would attend daily prayer meetings. Mac, who also missed having Tom in Cuzco, was keen to see the place for himself and so Tom suggested that Mac and Geraldine ride over there with him and Lily. Then if they wished, they could both travel further into the *Montana* – the rugged mountains. I happily agreed; Geraldine's enthusiasm was lovely, but sometimes she could be quite exhausting. However, if I had known what would happen while they were away, I would never have encouraged their little expedition.

The four of them set out on horseback with an Indian guide. Their path led over the green hills behind the city followed by a long and steep descent through a rough mountain gorge to the Vilcanote River. Following the course of the swiftly flowing icy stream, they passed through several villages before ascending again and reaching the few buildings which would become the main farm area of Urco. They all stayed overnight in a small inn and leaving Tom and Lily the next day, Mac and Geraldine continued with the guide and headed towards to mountains. The paths they travelled were narrow and quite overgrown in places. At the height of the snowline, the rarefied air made them breathless and the snow was dazzling in the brilliant sunshine. But at nights they were freezing cold.

Back in Cuzco I was enjoying some peace and quiet and having Peggy all to myself. She was six months old and such a lively little baby. So at first, I thought nothing of it; I'd had mild diarrhoea before. But the following day my temperature rose, the diarrhoea was worse and I began to feel distinctly unwell. I wished I hadn't sent the others off on their expedition. I thought I probably had developed dysentery and fearing for Peggy, I asked Sophia to fetch Flo Jarrett. When she arrived she took one look at me and sent me straight to bed and, just as I had done with her when Johnny was so ill, she moved into our house and took care of everything. Sadie helped as well by looking after Peggy and kept her away from me for fear of infection. Poor Sophia was distraught to see me so unwell, but she did as she was told.

The next few days were a complete blur. I had a persistent headache, my temperature kept rising and at times I was quite delirious. Sometimes I seemed to be walking down a long road bathed in light; it was so peaceful letting go, drifting. But then from time to time I would hear Peggy's cries and I found myself pulled back into the darkened room, my nightclothes drenched in sweat and my stomach knotted in pain. I didn't have the strength to make it to the pail-closet and had to struggle with a bucket by the bed. The stench was frightful but I was past caring. Days and nights of sweat and pain merged into one another. After four or five days, I was no better and the dreaded rose spots of typhoid appeared all over my distended belly. Through the mists I vaguely remember voices all around me and I learnt afterwards that they already feared the worst. By some miracle, John Jarrett managed to send word to Mac explaining how ill I was.

When they eventually heard the news, Mac, Geraldine and the guide rode through the night, mile after mile. Their legs were rubbed raw by the saddles and both riders and horses were so weary they often nearly fell; in spite of the layers of clothing they wore, strands of their hair became covered in frost. They hardly said a word to each other, since Mac's fear expressed itself through curt remarks and general irritability. By the time they reached the railway station at Asillo, Geraldine could barely stand. But at least they were there in time for the train from Arequipa which arrived the next morning. Gratefully they clambered aboard and slept most of the way to Checacupe. Geraldine told me later, that she had woken and recalled that it was now June 1st, and it was her nineteenth birthday. But, celebrating was the last thing on her mind. Tom met them with the fresh horses and again, saddle-sore they finally arrived at our house.

They were both truly shocked by what they saw; I had lost a lot of weight; my face was ashen grey and my dull eyes seemed to have sunk into their sockets; I was incoherent, rambling and tossing around in the bed. Flo was sitting beside me mopping my brow when they burst through the door and they said the look of relief on her face was palpable. Exhausted though she was, Geraldine immediately took her place, while John took Mac and Tom aside to explain the situation.

Flo returned to take care of her own children and Geraldine and Sophia took turns to sit with me for hours when they weren't minding poor little Peggy, who was completely confused by my delirium and by all the people who came in and out of the house. Days and nights blurred into one. I was convinced I was going to die and almost wished the end would come soon as the pains and fever were unbearable. Mac knelt several times each day beside my bed to say prayers but I don't recall him sitting with me for any length of time. He kept insisting that he had work to do despite Flo and John urging him to rest. He could never cope well with things which he couldn't control. At times he looked like a lost soul, and when I became more lucid, I felt guilty about the anxiety I must be causing him. But finally, I suppose God must have decided that my work on earth was not yet complete and slowly I began the long crawl to recovery.

CHAPTER 10

Cuzco and England. November 1907- September 08

It took many weeks before I began to feel anything like normal. I was very weak and quite exhausted after performing the smallest task. The worst part was the effect my illness had on Peggy. She had turned from a smiling, contented baby to a solemn and rather fractious one. Fortunately, Sophia had become quite adept at distracting her and much to my anxiety, sometimes Peggy quietened more quickly in her arms than she did in mine.

Geraldine already had a passage booked to return to England and after many discussions Mac agreed we should all return with her for our first furlough back home. We sailed in November 1907, just after my thirty-second birthday, and arrived back a couple of days before Christmas. I dreaded the seasickness I had suffered on the trip out here, but clearly all my years in smelly Cuzco had helped me develop a much stronger stomach! I was so excited to see the family again and show off my own baby. We stayed with my brother Sidney's family in Hampton Hill, not far from where I grew up. My nephew, Richard, was four and his sister, Kathleen, was just two and I had never seen either of them before.

It was wonderful to have clean sheets, a proper flush lavatory, and a hot bath – my first in three years! My sister-in-law, Millie, threw away nearly all my tatty, torn clothes and instructed her dressmaker to supply me with several new skirts, blouses and even new undergarments. Everyone fussed over Peggy and she was quite overwhelmed by the toys and dolls she received on her first birthday. She had learnt to walk while we were on the boat home and at Sidney's I was forever running after her as she trotted happily from one room to the next. Fortunately, the voyage had restored her to her former happy self. Millie coped admirably not only with our invasion but also when several of my other brothers and sisters came to visit. It was wonderful seeing Susannah again. She adored Peggy and confided that she was desperate to have her own child, having already experienced two miscarriages.

Everyone wanted to hear about our life in Peru. They were very shocked by the conditions we lived in as well as by the poverty and ignorance of the Indians and the prejudice and hostility of the Catholic priests. Because we had married so quickly and left for Peru straightaway, none of my family had really met Mac before. I prayed that they would like him and see the soft side of him which was sometimes hidden. Mostly he was very charming and courteous but if the conversation turned towards Catholicism, he would start to preach with a slightly raised voice, in his strong Scottish accent.

'You have to understand, Sidney, that Rome's insistence on the confessional has destroyed the sanctity of the home and the purity of womanhood. Across the hearth falls the black shadow of the priest, and every husband knows that the innermost thoughts of the woman he loves, and their most sacred relationships are laid bare to the prying eyes and impure questionings of the man who holds heart and conscience in his unclean grasp. His daughters are polluted before they reach womanhood by the filthy questions addressed to them by the priest under the cover of the confessional.'

'Yes Mac, I don't think Millicent and Susannah need to hear all the details,' I urged. But once started on a mission, Mac would rarely stop.

'Yes Beatrice, but it isn't just about the confessional. The whole morality is destroyed by the Church's teaching concerning sin. Indulgences can be bought for a few pence, or by kissing the toe of some image, or a prayer before a saint. What conception of sin can those people have when they are taught that it may be expiated by such trifling?'

Millicent stood up to clear away the tea things and Sidney made a great fuss of lighting his pipe. The room fell silent.

'Millie, shall we take the children to the park. I think the rain has all but cleared now.' I said brightly. Mac looked uncomfortable and on the pretext of having a letter to write, he strode out of the room.

I became quite edgy wondering what he might rant about next and felt relieved when he decided it was time to return to Peru. The only important issue Mac and my family did agree on, was that I should remain in England until I regained my weight and was sufficiently strong to cope with returning to Cuzco. I argued that I needed to return sooner since there was so much work to do but eventually I had to concede that I needed more time. Mac couldn't wait to return and so he booked his passage back to Peru and left at the end of February.

After the terrible snowstorms which hit the south of England in April, the summer of 1908 was warm and sunny. Richard, Kathleen and Peggy played all day long in the garden and although I felt guilty, it was blissful to sit in the shade watching them play while sipping my sister-in-law's homemade lemonade. It took me back to being a child sitting with Susannah under the willow tree in our garden in Hampton, playing with our dolls. In summer the garden used to be filled with the scent of roses and lavender and I recalled helping my father dead-head the spent flowers to encourage them to bloom again. And I read books, so many books! It was such a treat to read what and when I liked. In Cuzco there was never time for this luxury. I bought books to take back with me that one day Peggy would grow to love – *The Wind in the Willows*, Beatrix Potter, and *The Just So Stories*. Sidney was also a book lover and when the children were asleep I raided his bookcases and devoured Henry James, E.M Forster and even Conan Doyle.

I tried not to think of how envious the women of Cuzco would be if they saw me living such a different way of life. Every few days I wrote to Mac to give him all our news. In one of his replies he suggested that if I was now well enough I could make myself useful by raising some funds for the Missionary Union. Suitably chastened, I packed away the books and organised visits to a number of church groups to explain about our work and ask for contributions. It did me good, for it was on those occasions, talking about our work, that I really began to miss him.

In September Peggy and I set sail once more. The voyage was uneventful and for the first time I was able to arrive in Cuzco by train, since the last section of the railway had finally reached the city. Peggy was excited to see the llamas and alpacas from the train windows and the nearer we came to Cuzco the more I felt as if I was at last coming home to a city I loved, despite all the difficulties and memories of my illness.

Mac was so pleased to see us. He hugged me and then bent down to pick up Peggy and hugged us both together. Peggy looked a little confused but she did remember him. He helped us and our luggage (since I had brought many much-needed supplies) into a horse drawn carriage and as we trotted along I kept pointing out familiar sights to Peggy. But strangely we passed the turning to our house and continued up a steep hill on the west of the city.

'Where on earth are we going Mac? Please! I am really quite tired, Peggy is hungry and I just want to get back home.'

'Patience my dear,' Mac replied with a smile.

Eventually we arrived at a large two storied white house, built of adobe bricks with a corrugated iron roof. Mac helped us down from the carriage and led us towards the house.

'Welcome to your new home, my dear Beatrice. I have missed you so very much.'

'What do you mean Mac? Home? Why is this our home?'

'Last year, when you were so ill, I made a promise to myself that if you survived the typhoid and were willing to stay in Peru, I would build us a house. A house with its own fresh water supply, a proper bathroom, a view and a garden. It would be a place where we could all work and hold meetings away from the prying eyes of the priests, showing them that we mean business and are here to stay,' he concluded breathlessly. 'Tom and I have worked our socks off over the last few months building the house and I was determined that it would ready for your return. It is called Monjaspata, which means Monk's Walk. Come, let me show you inside.'

I was astounded. Tom and Mac had actually built the place. I had no idea that either of them even had the skills. With the help of a few Indians, they had made their own adobe mud bricks and had taught themselves all they needed to know. It looked enormous but was in fact two houses joined together under the one roof. We were in one half and soon the nurses, Miss Pinn and Miss Wahnrow, would move into the other half. Each house had eight rooms, all with windows which had been fitted with small panes of glass made from old spoiled photographic plates which gave it an old English appearance. In the room upstairs which was to be our bedroom, a door led out onto the balcony. I gazed in wonder over a lovely river valley in one direction and the cobbled streets of Cuzco in the other. And beyond Cuzco were my lovely snow-capped mountains, range after range, they faded in the blue distance.

'Look what Lily has done,' said Mac as he led me proudly from room to room. All the furniture from our old house had been moved but in addition there were colourful woollen blankets and rugs which I had not seen before. On the whitewashed walls were some lovely watercolour landscapes which Lily had painted herself.

'And look, Beatrice,' Mac said imitating a drum roll, 'here is the bathroom with fresh running water from our very own spring, as well as a proper flush lavatory which we sent for, all the way from Lima.'

Everything felt and smelt clean and new. I couldn't believe how much they had achieved as I walked from room to room with an enormous grin on my face. There was a small tug at my sleeve and I looked around to see Sophia. She was smiling and her cheeks were wet with tears. She had grown quite tall and now at age fourteen she was almost a grown-up. Her father had died while I'd been in England and so Mac had made sure that she would have a permanent home with us.

'Welcome to your home Señora McNairn, welcome, welcome,' she exclaimed, 'I am so happy to see you and little Peggy.' She held out her arms to take Peggy, who made a squeal of delight to see her. I embraced them both and soon I too had tears welling up.

'Come now ladies, I think we should all have a cup of tea,' said Mac.

The house was sited in five acres of ground and Mac explained his plans for further buildings which would include a school room, a meeting room and even a small hospital. Although in the carriage it had seemed quite a distance from the centre of Cuzco, it was in fact only a fifteen-minute walk, though it took longer on the way back, uphill!

Behind the house the ground sloped gently upwards and a stream flowed from a small stone-built channel. As Peggy toddled over to the stream and splashed her hands in the water, in my mind's eye, I could see the lovely garden

I would create, full of Peruvian lilies, lupins, orchids and beautiful magenta Inca bells. It would be our own garden; a place for peace and contemplation and a safe place for our children to play. It felt like a wonderful fresh start.

A few days after we returned Flo and John Jarrett organised a special evening service of welcome. I was overwhelmed by the greeting I received. The old meeting room back in the centre of town was more crowded than I had ever seen it. As I walked in, with Peggy toddling beside me, everyone got to their feet and applauded. So many of them thought that having returned to England after the typhoid, they would never see me again. I gazed around at the smiles and looks of joy and love on all their faces and I felt truly at home again. This was where I belonged, and although it had been lovely seeing my family back in England, I knew that I never wanted to be anywhere else.

Much had changed since I'd been away. Tom and Lily were now well established at Urco farm and dear Lily had given birth to a lovely baby boy named Ronald. They had been joined by Mr and Mrs Job. Sadly, Sadie and Fred Peters had decided to leave Cuzco altogether and set up a mission in Cuba. But Miss Pinn and Miss Wahnrow both worked tirelessly and soon there was a constant trickle of patients arriving at Monjaspata seeking their nursing skills. We were also joined by another Scot, John Ritchie, who had previously been based in Lima. He began to issue a monthly periodical in Spanish setting forth the gospel message. He established a bookstore and despite forceful opposition from Father Carrillo and his cronies, small groups were encouraged to gather regularly for "family worship". He clashed with Mac many times because he believed that giving people access to the written word which could be read and re-read in the privacy of their own homes was more useful than street preaching.

'You know it makes sense, Mac. You've seen it for yourself over and over again. The ignorant class is too fanatical to come and give us hearing, the student class considers Christianity a false and played out farce and therefore will not come. And the middle-class, who are more in sympathy with us, and to whom we more readily get access, dare not associate with us, less they lose caste, position or even business connections. The printed word can be taken home and read in private. The printed word spreads far and is read and re-read whereas the spoken word, heard by thirty or forty is half forgotten and usually gets totally distorted.'

'I agree John, but I think there is a place for both,' Mac replied. He was keen to return to his previous practice of riding out to the villages to preach to the Indians who rarely came to the city. I left them to it.

My own midwifery work continued much as before, though with Peggy being nearly two and a half, my days were very full and it soon became much more convenient to hold most of our meetings at Monjaspata.

On Wednesdays, we usually held a women's sewing group where middle-class women could come and work at some sewing together, have a cup of tea and enjoy some gospel reading. And once a month, in the evening, we started a social for the *muchachas*, or servant girls. They were all so young, although some of the older ones brought their babies. Sophia knew many of the girls and she helped prepare the food and join in the games. We began with games such as blind man's bluff, or musical chairs. What a sight they made, running about with their full skirts, and their brightly coloured shawls. I suppose they had seldom played in their lives; most of their days were sad and weary. After some games, we would give them tea and cakes, and however much we provided it all disappeared. After this Mac gave a magic lantern show and I always loved to watch the girls' looks of astonishment when they saw the pretty scenes of English life, and other pictures, thrown onto the sheet. We would end with some prayers and information about our other meetings and invite them all to return for the next social in a month's time.

Gradually we gained more and more converts and one bright, though chilly, Sunday morning, our little company of Christians wended their way to a secluded spot among the hills, where during one of the mountain torrents a deep pool had been formed. Several young men wanted to be baptised. The first, Juan, had been in the Franciscan monastery in Cuzco for three years, but instead of learning the ways of goodness and truth as he had hoped, he had been surrounded by nothing but immorality and vice. Sickened and disgusted with such a life and such companions, he left the monastery and obtained employment in our photographic studio. From there he came to the meetings and became a Christian. Another man, Lucas, who was once a church organist, had been attracted to come to our meetings by the singing he heard. Through his study of the bible he too saw the errors of the Catholic teaching. One evening instead of our usual preaching service, we had a testimony evening, when these young men and several others testified to the way they had been brought to Christ. It was so impressive and made us feel the value of our work. Those were such happy days.

Sadly, a month after my return, Florence and John Jarrett decided to relocate to Arequipa. A new couple, Mr and Mrs Sears, were due to join us as soon as they had completed their Harley College training in the New Year. It was such a shame to see Flo and John leave after all we had both been though. Finally, I felt I had been able to break through Flo's prickly exterior and I'd hoped we'd become lifelong friends. But as Mac explained, the important work for a missionary was not to become too settled in one place, but to establish a new mission, find enough converts to run it and then to move on to somewhere new. I hoped that this dictum would not apply to us. Having only just returned to Cuzco I had no intention of "moving on" but I kept my thoughts to myself.

CHAPTER 11

Cuzco. February 1909

Now that we lived at Monjaspata there was enough room for a large dining table, Mac was keen to entertain anyone who might have influence and be favourable towards our mission. Through Juan Rosaz, his university friend, he had met several other academics and professionals. A man he particularly liked was *Señor* Carlos Romero, a well-respected historian and archivist who spoke excellent English.

One weekend in February, we had an English couple, Colonel Percy Fawcett and his wife Nina, staying with us for a couple of days. Mac thought they might be interested to meet *Señor* Romero, and so on their last night he invited him to dinner. Colonel Fawcett, a military man in his late forties who had a bushy moustache twice the size of Mac's, had been commissioned to explore and make maps of the borders between Peru, Bolivia, and Brazil. Having recently finished the work, he and his wife decided to spend some time in Cuzco. They were a rather eccentric couple with many fascinating tales to tell and I was looking forward to the evening. However, at the last minute, *Señor*

Romero asked if he could bring along another guest, an American academic from Princetown, Professor Hiram Bingham, who had recently returned from making from an archaeological trip at Abancay.

'Oh Mac, I thought it was going to be a nice quiet evening with our guests and now we have an American professor to entertain as well.' I felt embarrassed, imagining that this professor would expect much more than we could offer.

'Don't be silly, it's only one extra person and he should be a very interesting man.'

'Yes but… won't they expect us to serve wine or *chichi* beer?'

'No Beatrice. No. There'll be no alcohol served at our table, not now, or ever. Our guests will drink our pure spring water just as we do.'

Fortunately, as well as Sophia, we now had a cook which relieved me of the harrowing task of having to produce something from my limited menu of "variations on stew" for these sophisticated guests. But in spite of not having to prepare a meal, I was nervous about how all the guests would get along with each other.

I need not have worried. The American professor and Colonel Fawcett found that they had much in common from their travels around South America and to begin with *Señor* Romero seemed content to make small talk with the Colonel's wife.

'What brought you to Cuzco, Professor?' I asked as we sat down to eat. He explained he was in Cuzco as part of an exploratory trip to Bolivia and Peru. He was a tall, good looking man of about the same age as myself, and seemed quite at ease with people he'd not met before.

'Well my companion, Clarence Hay, and I have been in the area for some weeks now, Mrs McNairn. When we first arrived in Cuzco we were just so bowled over by both the city and the incredible structure at Sacsayhuamán that we extended our trip to visit some ruins we'd been told about up near Abancay. The local prefect there, *Señor* Juan Nuñez, persuaded us to make the steep climb to a place called Choqquequirau, which means "Cradle of Gold".

'Ah yes,' interrupted *Señor* Romero, 'it is thought to have been the final refuge of the Incas when thousands of them hid there in the citadel to escape the Spaniards. It is assumed that it must be full of hidden treasure.'

'Did you find any treasure, Professor?' asked Mrs Fawcett.

'Of course much actual treasure in the form of gold and jewels was buried by the Spaniards themselves,' continued *Señor* Romero, before the professor had time to answer. 'Frequently they hid it in the thick walls of their houses, there being no banks or safe deposits. Then through death or other causes these hiding places were forgotten. Sometimes during the alteration or destruction of old buildings very valuable hoards have been brought to light. I came across one amusing example, just the other day. There was a gentleman who had moved into a large Spanish house of the colonial period and decided to do a bit of exploring. He went all over his house tapping the walls with the hope of discovering some *tapida*, as these hoards are called. One night, to his great delight and excitement, he found in one room a part of the wall which sounded hollow to his tapping. Getting some tools and a crowbar he attacked the wall, and sure enough his crowbar broke through into a cavity. He enlarged the hole sufficiently to enable to insert his arm and hand, and groping around he seized an object which proved to be an exquisite little golden image of pure Inca workmanship. Thrilled to the marrow he thrust his hand in again and pulled out another golden treasure. Presently he had quite a number of perfect and valuable examples of the finest Inca work. By now it was quite late and he decided he would wait until morning and take the whole wall down. He retired to bed, not to sleep, but to dream of untold riches.' *Señor* Romero, paused and took another mouthful of cook's delicious *Pachamanca*.

'What happened next?' asked Professor Bingham.

'Well, at last came the morning and he started work on the wall, but hardly had he begun, when he heard a clamour at the front door. He opened the door and was confronted by his irate neighbour from the adjoining house who wanted to know what the man thought he was doing, breaking through into his cupboards where he kept his lifetime collection of Inca curios and treasures! The poor man was so embarrassed and immediately had to set about repairing the damaged wall.'

We all laughed, in spite of what seemed to be a slight distraction from Professor Bingham's tale.

'So, returning to Choqquequirau, Professor, what did you find?' asked Mac.

'Well, just getting there was an adventure in itself. It rained and it rained. We crossed well-nigh impassable bogs, swollen torrents, avalanches of boulders, and traversed rivers by balancing on slippery logs. Most of the time we were hanging onto the side of a mountain almost by our eyelids. But what we found was just amazing. High above the Apurimac River, we did find the Inca ruins. Nowhere have I ever witnessed such beauty, such grandeur as was displayed here; the site is surrounded by snow-capped mountains, hills and tropical jungles. The Inca walls were mostly covered by vines but we could clearly see a large single storey structure with many doors and a block of two-storey houses with gabled ends. Sadly, *Señor* Nuñez, who'd been there before, had used dynamite in his efforts to search for treasure and we could see several areas which had been plundered. But what excited me most was finding some small cave-like tombs, not yet plundered, which contained many bones. I think I have probably discovered a very important archaeological site and I mean to return as soon as I can to excavate it more fully.'

'How exciting!' said Mrs Fawcett. 'Did you find anything else?'

'No gold or silver, I'm afraid, but I did find these two items of interest, hidden in a small niche and these give us some insight into how the people here lived and worked, don't you think?' He reached into a canvas bag by his chair and withdrew first a small stone bobbin of the sort I had seen local Indians use for spinning yarn and then a round cobble stone which he explained would have been used as a hammer.

'I know this is going to sound strange,' said Mrs Fawcett, 'but I have just remembered something. I have a great interest in the occult and before I came on this trip someone told me about an old woman who lives on Dartmoor who has the gift of second sight. I happened to be staying with some friends nearby and so I went to seek her out. After much mumbling, eventually the woman quite clearly told me, "I can see you are going on a long journey overseas, and will see strange places and things." Well that bit was fairly easy as I am sure I had mentioned my trip to her when I first arrived. But then she described all sorts of cities and so on that I would visit and finally she said, "I can see you now among the mountains; you are on horseback in a strange place. Yonder are jagged peaks; away below are the red roofs of a city. I see great stones piled one on top of another. Now I see you getting off your horse and entering a dark place. Be careful it is dark and steep." And now comes the interesting part.' Mrs Fawcett paused and looked around at as all. 'The old woman told me that I would find a great cave full of gold and that I would see people dressed in strange clothes wearing headbands made of crimson wool. At the time I dismissed what she said as pure fantasy, but now listening to you, Professor Bingham, perhaps there is something in what she said. We'd love to find some buried treasure, wouldn't we Percy?'

'Yes, my dear, but I fear we have run out of time. We leave for Lima tomorrow and then the boat back to England,' explained her husband.

'Well,' said Mac, 'I have heard many tales of treasures being concealed by the Incas, even as the invading Spaniards were already past the city walls. There are innumerable tunnels and labyrinths beneath Cuzco caused by limestone fissures which could hide any amount of treasure.'

'I believe they call those labyrinths, *chinganas*,' said Professor Bingham. 'My colleague, Clarence, was told about one which was thought to extend into the heart of the mountain and was said to communicate not only with the fortress of Sacsayhuamán but also with the city itself. Apparently two students took it upon themselves to explore and found themselves underneath the former Temple of the Sun where they could hear the chanting mass in the Church of Santa Domingo, which now stands in its place.'

'But what you are describing, Mrs Fawcett,' said *Señor* Romero, 'is the view from Sacsayhuamán. There you have the serrated mountain peaks surrounding the valley of the Vicanota; below are the red tiled roofs of Cuzco and the great stones piled on one another has to be the ancient fortress. It sounds as if the old woman of Dartmoor was correct.'

'Oh I wish I could stay longer and see it for myself,' said Mrs Fawcett. 'Professor Bingham, I do hope you will take time to find some of this golden treasure and send me just a few pieces. My friends back in England would be so envious.'

'It certainly sounds like it may be worth a look,' said the Professor. 'There is so much to see and explore, I think I could happily spend the rest of my life following up all these clues. I wish I, too, didn't have to leave so soon.'

I looked around the table at our dinner guests. They all seemed so well-educated, so well-travelled and so confident. Even though I had lived here in Cuzco, for nearly five years, I hadn't been anywhere else in Peru, let alone the rest of the world. I began to feel rather wistful until Mac brought me back into the conversation.

'I think Professor, I might have one more set of ruins you might want to explore next time,' said Mac. 'Beatrice, do you remember that old Scot who came to our house just before New Year?'

'You mean poor old Franklin. Of course, I remember him,' I replied. Turning towards the Professor I explained. 'Apparently he had come to Peru with another man many years ago, in search of a new life, but his companion sadly died and discouraged he had settled down among the Indians and lived their life. But now he knew he was coming to the end of his life and death was near. Somehow, he heard about us and came to our house. He died here and we buried him in the plot of land on the hill above Cuzco.'

'Indeed,' Mac continued. 'I had come across him a couple of years ago when myself and Tom Payne, a fellow missionary, were riding one day through one of those lovely valleys, and we came to a straggling Indian village. As we rode through the cluster of houses we saw an old man sitting in the doorway of a hut. He glanced up at us and after one strange look, turned his face away as if ashamed. As we rode on I said to Tom, "Did you see him? That was no Indian." Although he appeared quite dark skinned he couldn't have been an Indian because he had a long white beard.

So it was a complete surprise when a couple of months ago, that same old man turned up here, at Monjaspata. He had remembered us and something had stirred in the old man's heart; a desire to see his "ain folk" again and to speak in his "ain tongue" as we Scots say. But before he died he told us of some of his wanderings which might interest you Professor.

He told us that high above the Urubamba River across a gorge, he had seen fragments of old Inca buildings partially hidden by a jungle of vines and vegetation. He sincerely believed there must be some city there and begged us to go and explore.'

'Above the Urubamba River, you say? Do you know exactly where he meant?' asked Bingham taking out a small notebook.

'I think I might have a map somewhere.' Mac got up from the table and rummaged in a drawer.

'Wouldn't you want to go and find it for yourself Mr McNairn?' asked Colonel Fawcett.

'Well I suppose it might be fascinating, but you must understand that our work here is far too important to allow us the time to go searching for lost cities.' Not finding the map, he returned to the table and sat down.

'I remember he described the place quite poetically. He said something like, "I saw the fragments of Inca buildings quite clearly from the top of a mighty cliff, two thousand feet high, named *Mandor Pampa* above the roaring river of the Urubamba, and not far from the old hacienda of *Torontoy*." Perhaps somewhere else for you to explore on your next trip, Professor.'

'Indeed, indeed,' replied Bingham thoughtfully.

CHAPTER 12

Cuzco. 1909

Having spent so much time sitting in Sidney's garden when I was recovering from the typhoid, I couldn't wait to start creating a garden at Monjaspata. Mac left the planning entirely up to me; having worked so hard to build the house in the previous year he felt he had much more important tasks to do. The house he grew up in as a child in Edinburgh had a small strip of lawn at the back and he couldn't see the point of spending time cultivating flowers when vegetables would be much more use.

I began by clearing the larger stones and using them to mark out the flower beds. Peggy loved to try and help by collecting smaller stones in a little basket and then placing a small stone on top of my larger ones! Since so many people made their way up the hill to Monjaspata to seek the help of the nurses, Ethel Pinn and Edith Wahnrow, word got around that the *Señora* McNairn was constructing a garden and soon I had many offers of help from grateful patients. The soil in flower beds was dug over and raked smooth and an area to grow a few vegetables was walled off to one side. Outside the back door, on our side of the house, a pergola was erected, over which, I planned to grow purple bougainvillea and pale cream passion flowers. Underneath I placed a small wooden bench. I used to sit there in the late afternoon sunshine, with Peggy on my lap as I read her stories and taught her some of the names of the plants which would eventually fill the garden with scent and colour: alstromeria, amaryllis, geranium and cantua. I had so many offers of help; donations of seeds and small cuttings as well as some quite large well-established plants to give some instant growth and colour.

Mac sometimes reminded me that I was neglecting my mission duties but he could also see how contented I was, as I dug and raked and sprinkled water from the spring over my freshly planted seeds. The flow of our stream never varied, wet season or dry, and it seemed to come from the very heart of the hill. We made many enquiries as to the source of this perennial flow, but no one seemed to know. One day, however, an old Indian came to us and said he'd heard that we had been enquiring as to the origin of our precious water supply and he said he could help. As a boy, he remembered an outburst of water far up on the mountainside above our land. The authorities had set a band of Indians to dig down and find the source of the flow. They dug deep down and at last came to a great stone slab from beneath which the water was rushing. They raised the stone with great exertions and inside was a wonderful ancient construction. The old man told us that he had seen the water rushing through several stone channels which radiated into the mountain via a large central chamber. From this it flowed through another stone passage all the way down to the city. Apparently one part of the water flowed into the fountain in the Calle Hospital, and the other part ran into our little stream at Monjaspata.

This made both of us very curious and so with a few of the old man's friends, armed with picks and shovels, we climbed up to the spot the old man remembered. We found a deep hollow filled with shrubs and undergrowth and we could see some evidence of the long-ago excavation. The men cleared away the vegetation and Mac began to dig down. Eventually his pick struck the same stone slab and with great difficulty he levered it up wide enough to squeeze through the gap. Naturally I was not allowed to go further but the men took off their outer garments, shoes and socks and lowered themselves into the darkness and the water. They lit candles they had brought with them and found exactly what the old man had described. Meanwhile I waited impatiently in the sunshine to hear what they might find. After about thirty minutes I was relieved to see Mac's head poking through the opening.

'It's amazing Beatrice. I wish you could see it. There are three or four beautifully constructed tunnels, some two feet or more in height and about a foot wide and the water flows from the heart of the mountain into the lower chamber which is where we were standing. And there is another similar tunnel through which the water pours down towards the city.'

'So Mac, do you think this is where our Monjaspata stream comes from?'

'I don't see why not. I can't believe how well these channels have been constructed. They clearly date back to Inca times. The stones have been cut with mathematical precision and fitted together without mortar of any kind.

It's as good as the finest workmanship to be found in the Temple of the Sun itself, and all buried within the heart of the mountain.'

But because we still couldn't be sure that this was the source of our stream, the next day Mac returned up the hill and easing open the stone slab he poured some small pieces of cork and a bottle of crimson food colouring into the water. He had previously stationed one of the Indians at the fountain outside the Calle Hospital and myself and Peggy by the stream flowing through our garden at Monjaspata. After thirty minutes the man by the Calle Hospital ran back to tell me that the water in the fountain had run red with bobbing corks. But although I waited and waited, I didn't see a single cork or tinge of dye. The source of our little stream was to remain a mystery and it made my garden at Monjaspata extra special.

It wasn't until the middle of June that I realised I was three months pregnant. My periods had become so erratic following my illness that I had sadly imagined that I might never be able to conceive another child. I was so happy that at last Peggy would have a brother or sister to play with. Mac was overjoyed but immediately forbade me from doing any heavy work and chided me for not realising I was pregnant sooner, when I had possibly risked my health while heaving rocks and small boulders around in the garden.

'We must take great care of you Beatrice. I have a strong feeling that this one will be a boy and I wouldn't want you risking anything that might harm the welfare of my son,' he said firmly.

'Oh Mac! I understand your concern, but pregnancy isn't an illness. I'm still able to do most things and until Mrs Sears settles in properly I am still the most experienced missionary midwife.'

For the next few days I felt he was watching me all the time. If I went into the garden to pick some herbs for a meal he followed to make sure I didn't start pulling weeds. But one evening when Peggy reached up her arms to me wanting to be picked up, he said, 'No Peggy! Leave Mummy alone, you're a big girl now, and you don't need anyone picking you up.' Peggy let out a wail of frustration.

'Mac, this is ridiculous,' I replied, gathering Peggy into my arms. 'I know you are trying to be helpful, but you really have to trust me to know what I can and can't do.'

Of course I was anxious as well, and I wrote to Flo to ask if she might be willing to return to Cuzco when my time drew near, sometime in January. I knew I'd want someone I could trust to help me. She replied that she'd be glad to help. She also wrote that they had settled well in Arequipa and that they had been able to establish a small school; something we had always struggled with in Cuzco. They invited Mac to see how it was all going if he could make the time to take the train over to see them.

Mac gradually became more relaxed about my pregnancy and he often talked about his own childhood and the effect on him of losing his mother at such a young age. He wanted our son's childhood to be loving and secure and he even started imagining how he would follow in our footsteps and come to Peru to preach the gospel. When we discussed names, he favoured John, Charles, or Stuart, after both our fathers and himself, and although I kept reminding him that it could be a girl; somehow, we both became convinced he would be a boy. Meanwhile I continued to feel healthy and life carried on as it had before; visiting the sick, delivering babies, teaching people about our faith, and playing with Peggy in the garden which soon blossomed with flowers. Unlike my pregnancy with Peggy, this time I talked to my growing bump. I called it *Semilla* which is the Spanish for seed and most evenings when the day's work was done and Peggy was tucked up asleep, I wandered around my garden pointing out all the different plants to *Semilla* and urged him or her to grow as strong and healthy as the plants.

In mid-August, Mac decided to take the train to Arequipa and planned to stay there for about five days. Once again, I was glad to have the house to myself, apart from Sophia and the nurses next door. I dearly loved Mac, but sometimes his enthusiasm for the work became more like an obsession and he seldom seemed to relax and enjoy what we had achieved because he was already planning what must be done next.

He had been gone for three days when I woke in the middle of the night with awful cramping pains in my belly. I made myself some chamomile tea and for a while the pains went away. Just some indigestion I thought with relief. But two hours later the pain started up again and this time I knew I was having contractions. It was much too soon. I was only about nineteen weeks pregnant. It was still dark and at times the pains became so severe that I cried into my pillow not wanting to disturb anyone – besides, there was nothing anyone else could do. I got up, I lay down, I paced the room, massaging my belly and pleading with *Semilla* to settle down and stay safely within me.

And it seemed to work. The pains died down and when daylight came I was able to get Peggy dressed and give her breakfast.

'You look tired *Señora* Mac,' said Sophia. 'Are you not well?'

'No, I am fine, Sophia, I just had a bad night.'

We both went about our morning routines but when I asked her to go to the market she seemed reluctant to leave me.

'I go later.'

'No, Sophia, I'd like you to go now as there are other things I need you to do…'

I couldn't finish what I was saying; I doubled up in pain and felt a rush of blood on my thighs. I struggled to reach the bathroom and once there, I lay on the floor clutching my stomach. Peggy followed me and peered around the door looking so frightened. I shouted at her to go away. Suddenly, the room seemed full of people; Sophia and Ethel and Edith. Between them they helped me to my bed.

I knew then, for certain, that I was losing my baby.

Once again, something unbearable was happening to me and once again Mac was not with me. The day was a blur. Mrs Sears, my fellow midwife, was summoned but she had little or no experience of managing a late miscarriage.

The person who was the most help was Sophia. Taking Peggy with her she disappeared for a couple of hours and returned with a bunch of medicinal herbs which she brewed together into a rather foul smelling tea which she insisted I drank. The ancient Andean medicine helped with the pain and calmed me down. In my mind, I went over and over the past few weeks and tried to think what might have caused the miscarriage. Was it something I'd done while gardening? Was it anything to do with my typhoid illness? Why was God punishing me like this? Had I not suffered enough?

Someone sat with me all through the day and towards dusk, when I felt as if I couldn't bear the pain any longer, my tiny baby was born.

He looked just perfect. His whole body fitted into the palm of my hand. I searched every inch of him for an explanation. His hands were no bigger than my thumbnail. His eyes, just a crease under his forehead and he had a trace of smile on his little face. For a short while his heart was still beating and I cuddled him and kissed him and counted his fingers and toes again. Then his heart stopped and I knew it was all over. 'I'm sorry sweet baby, I am so sorry that I couldn't keep hold of you. Please forgive me and rest in peace.'

I was silent for a while as I cried softly and rocked him. Then, as my contractions started up again for the delivery of the placenta, Mrs Sears looked flustered. 'What do you want me to do with it?' she asked, trying to take him from me.

'He is not an "it" Mrs Sears!' I shouted. 'He is a person and he will have a name.' She sprung back as if she'd been slapped and ran out of the room, calling for Miss Pinn.

'What is it?' Ethel asked gently as she closed the door behind her.

'I'm sorry. I've just shouted at Miriam and I shouldn't have, but sometimes she can be so infuriating.'

Ethel calmly helped me to wrap him in one of Mac's handkerchief and place him gently in the small wooden bowl where I usually kept my hairpins. After she'd cleared everything away and put clean sheets on the bed, Sophia slipped quietly in to see me. But it was too much for the poor girl. She took one look at my infant and fled from the room.

Eventually I asked them all to leave me alone. Slowly I washed and dressed and wrapping my soft alpaca shawl around me, I left my baby safely in the bedroom and went into Peggy's room. Sophia had put her to bed and she was just drifting off to sleep. I sat with her for a while, stroking her hair, aching with grief.

There was no time to warn Mac. He was due back the following day; his train would arrive in the late evening. I was both longing to see him but also dreading his reaction to our loss. Should I show him the baby? Should I quickly bury him? Where on earth could I bury him and if I did, what if Mac wanted to see him? All day I worried and I still had a few cramping pains and some blood loss. I couldn't settle anywhere. Fortunately, Sophia kept Peggy entertained. The only thing I knew for certain was that I would not call my baby any of the names we had discussed. Instead I would call him "Peter", after Peter Pan, the boy who never grew up.

As the time for the arrival of Mac's train drew close, I kept wandering out into the darkness, straining to see his tall figure striding up the road towards me. I was upstairs checking on Peggy who had called out for me when at last I heard him entering through the front door.

'Hello Beatrice, I'm home,' he shouted putting his suitcase down noisily. 'Just wait till I tell you about what

John and Flo have achieved. It was very inspiring and I've come away with some excellent ideas.'

Peggy, hearing his voice called out, 'Dada, Dada!' I picked her up from her bed and carried her down to greet him, all smiles. He took her from me and bounced her up and down in his arms.

'Hello, young lady. Have you been a good girl?'

She giggled and nodded her head.

'Everything all right here?' he asked as he put Peggy down and took off his coat.

'Well…' I stuttered.

'That's good. I am really exhausted. Could you make me some tea, dearest?'

I settled a reluctant Peggy back in her bed and went into the kitchen to make us both some tea. Don't tell him too quickly I told myself. Give him time to settle down and tell me about his trip. We drank our tea and I watched his lips moving but I barely heard a word he said. Eventually when the flow of words trickled to a halt I said, 'Stay there Mac, I have something to show you.'

I went to fetch Peter in his little wooden cradle from our bedroom. Unable to find any words of my own, I knelt down beside Mac's chair and gently drew back the corners of the handkerchief.

'What on earth?'

'I am so sorry Mac.' I blinked back my tears. 'This is our baby boy. He came too soon.'

Mac looked once again. Spilling his tea, he pushed past me and rushed outside where I heard him vomiting.

I knew he'd be shocked and upset. But it never occurred to me that he might be revolted.

Gently I tucked the handkerchief back over Peter's tiny body and sat back in my own chair. I didn't know what to do and so I waited.

Eventually he came back into the house. He closed the door, muttered an apology and grabbing his suitcase went upstairs.

I was stunned. Angry. How could he say nothing? How could he not even ask how I was?

Taking Peter with me, I wrapped us both in my shawl and crept into the garden to try to calm down. I don't remember how long I sat there on my bench in the moonlight, crushed by sadness.

After an age, Mac came out to find me.

'I'm sorry Beatrice. I'm sorry I wasn't here for you. Why don't you leave, this …' he pointed at Peter, 'and come to bed now. We are both tired and overwrought.'

'He is called "Peter". I have called him Peter. He was our son and you can't even look at him.'

Mac said nothing, patted my shoulder awkwardly and retreated inside. I remained sitting on the garden bench. Moths fluttered through the foliage and bats swooped around the trees. Then it came to me. It was as if this spot in the garden, on the far side of the stream, had been waiting for something special. Taking a small trowel, I knelt down on dry earth and with tears running down my cheeks, I dug and dug, tossing the earth aside. Then, I buried my baby, still wrapped in the handkerchief, deep in the ground. I placed a large flat stone over the earth and laid a posy of flowers on it. When I slipped into our bed some while later, Mac was already asleep.

The following morning, he woke before I did. He got Peggy washed and dressed and helped Sophia with breakfast. 'How are you feeling, dearest?' he asked when eventually I appeared.

I managed a weak smile.

'I don't want you to worry Beatrice. I will sort out exactly where and what we need to do with the baby. Sorry. I mean with Peter.'

'You needn't bother. I want him to stay close to me so I have already buried him on the far side of the stream. I don't suppose you want to see, do you?'

'What do you mean, you have already buried him? Did you not think I might want to have a part in it?' he hissed. 'Sophia, keep Peggy inside for a few minutes please.' Grabbing my arm, he propelled me into the garden. 'Show me! I want to see what you have done with *my* son.'

'But last night you wouldn't even look at him. The sight of him made you physically sick and anyway, he was *our* son and you weren't there.'

'It was such a shock, Beatrice, and I have already apologised.'

Stung by each other's words, we fell silent as we looked down at the bare earth and the stone and the posy of flowers. Then Mac dropped to his knees and pulled me down beside him.

'Dear Lord, we do not presume to understand Thy mysterious ways. Grant us the courage to bear our suffering just as your Son also bore his suffering for all of our sakes.'

How could I possibly tell him that I didn't want prayers? I wanted to weep. I wanted him to hold me, soothe me. But I felt too angry, too beaten.

CHAPTER 13

Cuzco. Sept 1909 – June 1910

Somehow, we got through the days and weeks, unable to comfort each other but with no more harsh words. I was certain that Mac blamed me for my miscarriage because I had overdone things when I was first pregnant, and since I too, wondered if it was my fault, there seemed little point in discussing it further. I saved the posy of flowers which I had put on Peter's grave and pressed the fragile blossoms between two sheets of blotting paper to keep them safe. I hid them in a small box, tied with a blue ribbon.

On the surface, I appeared to be coping; I did all the chores; I took care of Peggy; I took part in the bible study sessions and hardest of all, I delivered other women's healthy, although often unwanted, babies. But on the inside, I felt as if I was drowning. Why me, I asked God? But God never gave me an answer.

The only person who seemed to understand was Tom who was in Cuzco on a visit.

'I know how much you are hurting Beatrice and I know Mac is as well, although he'll never admit it. But plunging yourselves into work isn't going to take your pain away.

Why don't you bring Peggy and come and stay with Lily and me at Urco for a while?'

'That's kind, Tom, but I can't neglect my work here. It wouldn't be fair on Mac or the others.'

But I was torn. It was silly; part of me wanted to stay near to Baby Peter and part of me wanted to be as far away as possible. Much to my surprise, Mac strongly supported the idea. I suppose he didn't really know how to deal with me and so it was all arranged. Urco was about twenty miles away on horseback. It was the furthest I had been away from Cuzco, apart from my trip to England, in the all years we had lived there. So, a few days later, with Peggy balanced in front of me clutching the horse's mane, a mule behind bearing our luggage and Tom leading the way we set off. Peggy was so excited riding the horse that I felt my spirits lift as we left the streets of Cuzco behind us. The path led over lush green hills before descending steeply through a rough mountain gorge carved by the swiftly flowing Vilcanote River. Following the course of the river we passed through several small hamlets before reaching Urco. All along the way we came across numerous little companies of Indians, driving their llama flocks or mules, laden with merchandise and fruit. Some smiled at us and their women lifted their broad brimmed hats to wish us good day

We reached the farm in the early evening and Lily, with their baby Ronald, now eighteen months old, ran out to greet us. It had been a long day in the saddle, Peggy had fallen asleep several times and it had been quite an effort to prevent her from tumbling off the horse. But as soon as I dismounted I felt a renewed energy. The air felt so clear and as inhaled a deep breath I knew that Urco was a place where I could mend.

I didn't really know Lily. All the while she'd been settling into her new life in Peru, I'd been preoccupied with recovering from typhoid and then convalescing in England. Over supper, the love she and Tom had for each other could be seen in every gesture, every look. Clearly the life out here suited her. The pale complexion that she'd had when she'd arrived now bore a healthy tan; her fine clothes now changed for a sensible workaday skirt and blouse.

That night I slept soundly for the first time since Peter's birth and by the time I made my way downstairs the following morning, everyone, including Peggy had been up for hours. The large kitchen living room had similar décor to Monjaspata; sheepskin rugs, colourful woollen throws and delicate watercolours.

'Let me make you some breakfast,' said Lily looking up from where she was supervising Peggy and Ronald playing with wooden bricks on the floor.

'Thank you, Lily. I am actually quite hungry this morning, in spite of that wonderful meal you gave us last night. And I don't think I ever thanked you properly for all the beautiful paintings and rugs you gave us to decorate the mission house. You are a talented artist.'

Lily got to her feet, came over to where I stood and gave me a hug. 'It was a pleasure, though it was quite a risk, taking decisions about another woman's house. I am so glad you liked it.'

'Where is Tom?' I asked.

'It's harvest time, and one of our busiest, so he'll be out

there with Alan Job somewhere, supervising the Indians.'

'I know absolutely nothing about farming. What do you grow here?'

'We have already reaped small quantities of linseed, peas, beans, and barley but the main crop is maize. It is so busy that poor Tom scarcely seems to have closed his eyes at night time when the bell sounds for us to be up. The Indians start work at first light to get as much done before the sun overpowers them with its heat and glare. At the moment, we have around fifty Indians working for us every day, and some of the women help Mrs Job and me to prepare a breakfast for them of hot coffee and bread. They get the same in the evening and then we all join together for prayers. The deal is that they don't get paid until the very end of the day, after the prayers. Tom calls it his spiritual harvest.' She laughed and cleared my plate and cup from the table.

'Whoops a daisy!' she exclaimed sweeping Ronnie into her arms as Peggy gave an enormous wail and ran to me. Ronnie had just knocked down her carefully built tower of bricks. 'Come, let me show you around and keep these two from fighting each other.' Lily led us from the cool dark of the kitchen into dazzling sunshine. I had been too tired to appreciate the view when we'd arrived the previous evening. The farm buildings were sited on a plateau high above the river and the land all around it was terraced. Beyond, the snowy mountains seemed as if they were floating in a deep blue crystal sea. Their rugged slopes, splashed with sun, looked only a stone's throw away.

Lily explained how the terraces which they still cultivated were yet another ingenious invention by the Incas. Steep slopes were converted into flat areas which could be planted with crops and surrounded by stone walls. The stones retained the heat of the sun during the daytime and so the soil was protected from the frost and cold overnight. Walls were also built to channel the rainwater and prevent it from washing everything away down the slopes.

We walked past several outbuildings and a large barn to a nearby field. It was a glorious sight – a huge acre field, filled with maize, one dazzling mass of colours. Purples, pinks, browns, deep mauves, gold and sunny yellows. In one corner sat three small children in bright rags of clothing. They gazed at us and responded with wide smiles to Lily's wave.

'First the maize has to be cut in the terraced fields down there,' Lily pointed down the valley. 'And then it's brought back up here to the drying yard.'

'It looks like really hard work,' I said.

'Oh it is. Just imagine climbing a hill of nearly three hundred feet with a load of maize on your back, and then down again for a further load, and so on all day. Once it is cut it has to be husked and then sundried in that field for about three weeks,' she explained. 'We pray it won't rain in the next week or so while it's drying as that could ruin the crop. Once it has dried, the Indians will wait until nightfall for the maize to be quite cold before they put in the storage sheds. It must be cold so that it won't steam and become a hotbed for any sort of insect.'

'Goodness me. I hadn't realised the size of the farm here at Urco. You and Tom have achieved wonders.'

'Well, there is plenty more to do and now we also have Mr and Mrs Job helping us. We have the beginnings of a school and at the weekly bible study sessions we speak to them in Quechua, Spanish and English. But Tom is sometimes a bit like your husband, impatient for change and forgetting that these things take time.'

At her mention of Mac, I was shocked to realise that I hadn't given him a single thought since leaving Cuzco the previous day. He had seemed so distant, so cold, in the past few weeks that I had assumed he was still angry and disappointed with me. If only he could have talked to me about how he felt.

For the first few days at Urco I wandered along the many different paths that wound down to the valley or up into the hills behind the farm. Lily insisted that she take care of Peggy and that I should take some time for myself. Dearly though I loved Monjaspata, privacy was a luxury and time on my own was what I had been missing. Those days of solitude were wonderful. There was something so healing in the act of walking on my own, with no real sense of purpose other than simply being alive in a beautiful place and putting one foot in front of the other; connected to myself; connected to trusted friends; connected to the world.

At times on my wanderings I wept loudly, knowing that the wind would carry my cries away, relieved that no one would be upset by my tears, or tell me to think of others less fortunate than myself, or worse still, tell me that I would have plenty more babies in the future, as if losing a baby was no more than losing a favourite keepsake.

Lily said none of these things. She watched and waited until I was ready and one evening when the children were asleep and Tom was busy with some paperwork, she gently asked,

'Beatrice, I've been wondering about how you are feeling and whether you might like to tell me about Baby Peter?'

'Oh Lily, dear Lily,' I replied, my eyes already filling, 'you are the only person who has asked me anything about him.'

And she listened intently while I told her about his birth, his death and Mac's reaction to seeing his tiny body. It was a relief to talk about my baby but I felt rather guilty for telling her about how Mac had behaved.

'It has been so hard ever since. Mac simply won't talk about it and the few times I have tried, he says we must both heal ourselves through prayer and faith. Tell me Lily, how can I, a missionary's wife, admit to anyone that I am questioning what feels to me like God's cruelty, in taking away my son?'

'I don't have any answers about how God works but I do think it is important to be able to talk to someone human about the things in life which are so awful or are so hard to bear. The trouble with men is that they are brought up to show no signs of weakness or emotion. They pretend to feel nothing and consequently they are quite useless when they are confronted by women like us.'

I laughed. 'It's such a relief to hear you talk like this.' I already felt better having told her about Peter. 'But I can't get away from the thought that I am letting Mac down. I haven't given him the son he longs for; I'm neglecting my work because my heart isn't in it; I shouldn't be criticising him to you and I just don't think I am being the good wife I promised him when we married.'

Now Lily laughed. 'You mean you aren't a saint! Oh goodness me, how could I have been so mistaken? Welcome to the ranks of "ordinary-good-enough women". But seriously, Beatrice, if I hadn't had a good woman friend to talk to when I was married to my first husband, I don't think I could have survived.'

'You weren't happy together?'

'I did try. I really did try to be a good wife. I promised to honour and obey and do my duty. My mother told me that I would learn to love him. But love is not enough in marriage, there must be respect as well. How could I respect someone who treated me like a piece of his property, who took every opportunity to humiliate me in front of his friends, who forbade me from having friends of my own, not to mention his extremely distasteful bedroom habits?'

'You poor thing, and you were married when you were quite young I believe?'

'Yes, my parents decided that Tom was quite unsuitable as he had no money or title and the wonderful Maurice Murphy had it all. How furious Maurice would be to know that most of his money is now keeping me blissfully content as a missionary farmer's wife in the wilds of Peru!' she giggled.

And then we were both laughing. I laughed as I hadn't done for years, not since Susannah and I were in our teens when we tormented one of our tutors. We were both still laughing when Tom poked his head round the door to see what all the noise was about and when Lily tried to explain but couldn't get a sentence out, Tom joined in as well until the three of us were doubled up.

When we finally all calmed down, I embraced them both, 'You are the dearest friends anyone could wish for.'

I stayed at Urco for several weeks. Each day I suggested

to them that I should return to Cuzco and each day they urged me to stay just a little longer. Lily would examine both my cheeks and declare that they still needed a spot more colour. I was amazed that someone as young as Lily at just twenty-seven, had such a wise yet light-hearted attitude to life. When she had time, she would walk with me and we talked about anything and everything; our marriages, our families, our faith and our futures.

One morning, having left our children in the care of Mrs Job, we climbed a path which led quite far up into the hills. The air was clean and crisp and we stopped frequently to catch our breath and admire the view. One of the places we stopped was beside a tiny thatched hut which stood near the shore of a small lake. An old man was leaning on a stick by the door and he gestured to us to approach. He was joined by a woman who on seeing us fetched some sheepskins and ponchos and laid them on the ground for us to sit on. She muttered something in Quechua to the man and disappeared into the hut. Soon she returned with a dish of hot potatoes and another of grilled fish and invited us to eat. We knew that they were poor but they would be most offended if we refused their hospitality. Two small children emerged from the hut and clutched at her skirts, eying us half in fear and half in wonder, though very soon, Lily, speaking to them in their own language, had them giggling with delight. I felt nothing but admiration by the generosity of this family who had so little but gave us so much.

And so I returned home and picked up the threads of my marriage. Tom had helped me to understand that Mac was indeed grieving for our lost child and how he masked it with the traditional British stiff upper lip. He told me how Mac had spoken about me endlessly when he and Tom were building Monjaspata and how frightened he'd been of losing me when I'd so nearly died of typhoid.

I could see that Mac was glad to have me back, though for a while he was wary of upsetting me. But there was a tear in the fabric of our marriage which never mended properly. Of course, Sophia and Peggy were overjoyed to be reunited. Gradually I began to enjoy my work again and took extra care to continue to visit women who lost babies through miscarriage or stillbirth for many weeks after their loss. I tried to give them the care and support that Lily had given me.

One day, at the start of 1910, Mac returned from the post office waving a letter.

'Look, Beatrice. At last it's going to happen. The conference they have been planning is finally going to take place.'

I looked up from the dress of Peggy's I was mending and took the letter which Mac thrust under nose.

'"*The World Missionary Conference will take place at the Assembly Hall of the United Free Church of Scotland, Edinburgh on June 14th 1910. The aim of the conference is to make plans for a new and concerted approach to missionary work in the entire world. Missionaries are invited to submit comprehensive reports of the work they are undertaking which will be read out and discussed by all attendees. The conference will be presided over by Lord Balfour and chaired by John R. Mott.*"'

'That's wonderful. Will you be able to attend?'

'No I don't think so. We aren't due furlough until next

year, but I shall certainly give them a very detailed report, focussing not so much on what we have already achieved, but on how much more we need to do, but cannot do, unless we have better funding.'

For the next few weeks Mac spent almost every evening writing and rewriting his report. Our fellow missionaries were only too grateful that he took on this task. After several hours of scribbling and tearing up of paper he would stand up, stretch his back and say; 'Listen to this bit, Beatrice. Do you think this sounds all right?

"Exploited, oppressed, robbed, degraded, and brutalized to an almost unbelievable extent, the Indian has become apathetic and hopeless in his misery and helplessness. He takes comfort from the cocaine extracted from the coca leaf which he chews for its anaesthetic effect upon his hungry stomach and weary muscles, as well as for its deadening effect upon his mental sensibilities, enabling him as it does, to mechanically and unthinkingly accomplish long and burdensome tasks with but little nourishment.

His one relaxation is the exhilaration of getting beastly drunk on feast days and other special occasions. Indians must hear the message, for few can read but sadly their minds are thus too often dulled to take in our message. Cuzco's only hope is to be rid of Romanism with its unholy priests who hold absolute power.

And what is more, hospitals are full of people with smallpox, typhoid, consumption and the dire diseases which come upon men and women who habitually break the 7th commandment of adultery. Even the priests boast about how many young girls' lives they have ruined."

After the few attempts I made at suggesting alternative

phrasing, I learnt that what he craved was not constructive criticism but unbridled praise! Fortunately, the strain of his endless pacing and proclaiming was interrupted by a letter from my sister, Susannah, telling me she had given birth to a lovely baby girl and had named her Beatrice. In spite of my own misfortune, I was overjoyed for her and immediately wrote to her to ask for a photograph of my little namesake.

However, at the end of May, it seemed that all our efforts to bring the Word to these people were quite in vain. Despite submitting his comprehensive report, we learnt that South America, an entire continent, was to be excluded from the considerations of the conference as it was deemed not a legitimate "missionary" operation any more than Catholic Europe. Indeed, they pronounced it quite adequately card for by "our sister church of Rome".

I was sorely disappointed. Mac was furious.

Since there was no more we could do, we soldiered on with our work. I delivered more babies; we gained more converts; I tended my garden and we both enjoyed watching Peggy grow and learn about life. We saw Lily and Tom whenever we could and for a long while I was quite contented.

CHAPTER 14

London. May 1911

And then we came home. Or rather we left home; the home which Mac and Tom had built, brick by brick; the home which Lily had helped to decorate and furnish; the only home that Peggy had ever known. And I left behind my garden. The garden, which I had created and tended and watched blossom; the garden where baby Peter was buried. And we left Tom and Lily. And all our friends. And the nurses. And Sophia. We left the narrow, cobbled streets filled with ghosts of the Incas. We left the markets full of noise and smells and colour; the terraced hillsides of potatoes and maize; the sun-splashed red tiled roofs of the town. We left the distant snow-capped mountains and the clear blue air of Monjaspata.

And we returned to England, where we, as a couple, had never had a home.

It had always been our plan to return to England in the spring of 1911 for a three- month furlough. Most missionaries had leave every third year. So, I packed only the minimum we would need, leaving space to bring back more bibles and medical supplies. I was really looking forward to seeing my family and all the little ones, especially my namesake, baby Beatrice. By now Peggy was four and a half and we whiled away many hours on long the voyage reading stories about Mole and Ratty and Peter Rabbit. By the time we arrived in England, Peggy was already quite adept at picking out the letters and reading the shorter sentences.

We stayed at first with Susannah and Leonard in Twickenham where he and his brothers ran a grocery business. Mac stayed with us for a week before going up to Liverpool to attend the annual Keswick Convention, where he had planned to deliver the paper which had been excluded from the Edinburgh conference the previous year. Having only just arrived in England after such a long journey, we agreed that I would not to join him but spend time with Susannah instead.

It was three years since I'd seen Susannah and the first time I'd seen her as a mother of a lively one-year-old. She looked tired but had a calmness about her which reassured me that she was content. She wore her thick curly hair in a bun on the top of her head but as always, had several tendrils which escaped from the mass of pins aimed to keep them in place. I had always envied her thick hair, since mine was always fine and straight. She helped Leonard in the shop whenever she could and had a wonderful relationship with all their regular customers.

A week or so later Mac returned from Keswick full of excitement. After dinner, when the children were asleep and the others had retired for the night he told me about the conference.

'It's going to be a whole new start, Beatrice. A number of us have come together and we have formed a new organisation, quite separate from the RBMU (Regions Beyond Missionary Union), who in their ignorance believe there is simply no need for missionaries to work in Catholic countries. We are calling it "EUSA", the Evangelical Union of South America and to begin with it will combine the missions working in Argentina, Peru and Brazil. At last, Beatrice, we will have the freedom to develop the work as we see fit. We can establish bookshops, evangelical bible schools, and many more medical services.'

'That sounds wonderful, Mac. I'm so glad all our work has been taken seriously at last.'

'But that's not all. Because of my experience in the field I've been asked if I would take on the full-time role of secretary to act as a fundraiser and co-ordinator of all the mission activities in the different countries.'

'But I don't understand Mac. It is very gratifying that you have been asked to take on this role, but what does that involve? How on earth can you do all that on top of our work in Cuzco?'

'Ah, well,' he paused and looked a little sheepish. 'The job will be based in London at the new headquarters of EUSA, once we find some suitable offices.'

'What do you mean "the job is based in London"? What about our life and work in Peru?'

He remained silent, avoiding my gaze and fiddled with some papers in his briefcase. I felt a dark hollow developing in the pit of my stomach.

'Surely you aren't going to accept it, are you? Mac, are you seriously telling me you have already accepted this post? Did you not think of asking me first?'

'I'm sorry Beatrice, but sometimes in life, men must

make their own decisions about complex issues concerning the future welfare of their families. If you had joined me at the conference, you might have been involved in some of the discussions but since you chose to remain here with your sister, I'm afraid you will have to live with the consequences.'

I felt as if I'd been slapped.

'That is not fair. We agreed I would remain here but if I'd known this was going to happen, of course I would have been there with you. Although from the way you are talking it sounds as if my presence wouldn't have affected your decision.'

An angry silence filled the room. Mac continued to flick through his papers and I sat quietly, too stunned to talk.

When I couldn't bear the silence anymore I asked, 'But it doesn't have to be immediate does it? Please tell me that we can go back home, pack our things up properly and say goodbye to everyone, can't we?'

'No dear, that's out of the question. Two return fares would be a ridiculous expense at this time when the organisation is just starting up. I will write to Tom and explain everything and once we are settled here we can send for our things.'

'I can't believe that I am never going to see it all ever again. It seems so cruel.'

'I'm sorry that it's come as such a shock. I'm sure we'll go back there one day. But you've always known that true missionary work involves moving from place to place, and quite honestly, Beatrice, I am disappointed in you. As my wife, your duty is to support me, and I actually thought you'd be as pleased and enthusiastic as I am about this new chapter in our lives working for God.'

I knew better than to argue with that trump card. I had noticed that over the years, it was always "God's will" whenever Mac wanted his own way.

For a while all I could hear was a voice inside me screaming 'What about me? What do I want?' I tried to calm myself but couldn't hide the edge of sarcasm in my voice,

'Since I am unlikely to be able to practice midwifery, do you have any suggestions as to how I should occupy myself?' I tried to imagine myself reduced to being the little do-gooder wife who performs charitable works and sits in stuffy rooms with other women, sipping tea and discussing acceptable topics.

He gave me a withering look and said we would discuss it in the morning. We made our way upstairs to my sister's spare bedroom in a frosty silence. He patted my shoulders as I sat brushing my hair. I flinched.

'Come now, Beatrice, I know you are upset and disappointed,' he said as he climbed into bed. 'But I see a bright future for us. Peggy needs to start in a proper school soon.' He paused and when I made no reply said, 'I've been thinking for a while that she shouldn't be an only child, and perhaps it is high time we gave her a little brother – or sister,' he added hastily.

'I am sure you are right dear, but I have one of my beastly headaches coming on and I need to try and go to sleep.'

I too had been thinking about Peggy being an only child. I knew that I had benefitted from having so many brothers and sisters while I was growing up; the house was always filled with noise and laughter, except on Sundays when we were expected to be quiet. In the months since I'd lost Peter, I had claimed many headaches or other excuses to avoid any risk of falling pregnant again. But Mac was right. I didn't want him to be right. But perhaps if I did have another child I would have a new focus for this new life we were about to lead.

CHAPTER 15

London 1911

Mac wrote to Tom to explain what had happened but I wrote separately to Lily. Unsurprisingly, the letters back from them had quite different tones. Tom offered congratulations for Mac's new important role but Lily's letter to me was full of sympathy and sorrow about my being so far away. I also wrote to Ethel Pinn with a list of everything I needed her to parcel up and send to me. I hated the thought of her having to go through all my private things but I had little choice. I could tell from the responses from the Sears and Ethel that they felt abandoned by us and Peggy kept asking for Sophia. How could I explain that she would never see her again?

We had very little money and no possessions but by great good fortune Susannah knew of a family nearby who were travelling abroad for a few months, and who willing to rent us their house while they were away. If it hadn't been for my sisters I don't know how I would I have coped. Both she and Millie were very generous and helped me out with cast off clothes for both Peggy and myself. Gradually I learnt how to cook in the English style, but I really missed the spices, the brightly coloured maize cobs, and the variety of little knobbly potatoes I was so used to cooking back home. I continued to think of Monjaspata as home for many months.

Through the hot summer of 1911, the hottest I'd ever experienced in England, I still couldn't believe that we weren't going back. It was just like the time we had been in Twickenham before, when I was recovering from typhoid, as if we were on an extended furlough. I kept thinking, when I get back, I must start up the reading group for women again and perhaps a bible study group for new university students. And then I'd remember – we weren't going back.

'What on earth am I going to do with myself, especially once Peggy starts at kindergarten?' I asked Mac one morning.

'I think you will have quite enough to do looking after the house and taking care of Peggy. Why do you need anything else?'

'But Mac, I need to feel useful. In Cuzco I was a midwife and a nurse; I held bible study groups, I looked after our child, Sophia, the house as well as everything else.'

'Yes, Beatrice, but need I remind you that out there we had Sophia and a cook and in our present circumstances we simply can't afford that sort of luxury.'

There was nothing I could say.

Later that morning he said, 'Actually Beatrice, I do have an idea about how you could be useful. If you could learn to use one of those new-fangled typewriters you could assist me by typing up my lecture notes while I dictate them.'

So, he applied for funds to buy a brand new Remington

Standard typewriter and I attempted to master the keys. After a while, because my typing was so slow, Mac took to writing out his notes by hand and I typed them up afterwards once Peggy was in bed. This avoided his impatience at my slowness when he dictated but still won his annoyance as the clatter of keys disturbed his thinking. It didn't seem to occur to him that so much time could be saved if he learnt to type himself.

He was busy most days setting up the EUSA offices in central London and organising a tour of England to give lectures to raise funds for the mission. So, Peggy and I explored all the places I had loved as a child and we often had picnics in Richmond Park or by the Thames. Sometimes we were joined by Millie with Richard and Kathleen, my niece and nephew who were only a few years older than Peggy. Slowly I became resigned to the fact we here to stay.

One morning in late September after I had taken Peggy to kindergarten, there was a knock at the door. Mac was away in Exeter giving a talk and I had planned to give the kitchen a thorough clean up. The postman handed me a parcel wrapped in thick brown paper and tied with string. I read my name in Ethel Pinn's familiar flowing handwriting. At last my possessions from Peru had arrived. I tore off the paper and string to reveal my beautiful pale grey alpaca shawl folded around a battered cardboard box. I held the shawl to my face and tried to recapture the unforgettable smell of a new baby.

Carefully I opened the box. On the top was the slim volume of Wordsworth poems which Mac had given me that first Christmas. Had I really asked Ethel to send me that? Underneath was a small flat box tied with a pale blue ribbon. I knew what was in it and I had to steel myself to lift the lid. Inside, with petals so faded and fragile, was the posy of pressed flowers from Peter's grave. I closed the box and put it to one side.

Next was an envelope with a dozen or so photographs which I fanned out over the kitchen table. There I was, nearly ten years ago, looking most serious, in my ridiculous missionary training uniform; a smocked grey dress with puffed sleeves and a starched collar which chafed my neck. I'd been so proud to wear it at first, but it was so uncomfortable and what's more we had to wear thick woollen stockings in both winter and summer. I discovered very quickly how unsuitable it was for the sunny climate in Peru. Another photograph showed Mac as a dashing young man with friendly eyes and a handlebar moustache. No wonder all the girls fell for him! There was Peggy as a small child, sitting on a heap of drying corncobs at Urco, as well as various pictures of Cuzco and the garden at Monjaspata. I looked through them over and over again searching for something which was so familiar and yet seemed so terribly far away.

I was so excited I couldn't wait to show everything to my sister and as soon as Peggy had finished school I took her over to Susannah's house. It was the first time I'd been able to convey anything of what our lives in Peru had been like. We looked through the photographs and Peggy chipped in telling her all sorts of stories about our life in Cuzco.

'Have you got an old grocery box you don't need, that I can keep all these bits in?' I asked.

'I have something much better than that. It's just what

you need,' she said and hurried out of the room. She reappeared bearing a large wooden chest with a hinged lid covered in a faded tapestry which she plonked down on the floor.

'You do remember this, Beatrice, don't you?'

'It does look vaguely familiar. Where did it come from?'

'It used to be our mother's. It always sat under the window in the drawing room. It was full of cotton reels, coloured ribbons and embroidery threads. Don't you remember how we used make up stories about which colours she would have liked the best?'

'Well, I can't possibly take it from you.'

'No. I really want you to have it. It's no more mine than yours and I think it's time you had something from our past for yourself.'

When Leonard had finished in the shop he carried the chest back to our house and after I'd shown Mac some of the treasures, I wrapped them all up in the shawl and put the chest at the back of a cupboard in our bedroom. Dearly though I wanted to look through it every day, I knew that it would not help me to dwell too much on the life I felt I had lost.

As a distraction, one day I took the train up to London and went to visit my old stomping ground in the East End. Nothing much had changed apart from the occasional motor car chugging down the centre of the road. On the steps of the church we used to attend I was stopped by a thin woman in a much-darned coat offering me a leaflet. It had "Votes for Women" in big capital letters on the front. I was about to push pass her in the way I had learnt to avoid persistent peasants in the Cuzco marketplace, when she tugged at my sleeve and looked me in the eye.

'Please mum, please would *you* sign this petition to give women the vote?'

For a moment, I was quite taken aback. Why had she emphasised the word "you"? I looked at her again. There was something about the woman that looked slightly familiar.

'Don't you remember me, mum? I've grown up a bit but I was only fifteen when you delivered my first babe. I've never forgot how kind and gentle you were with me. It was near enough eight years ago and you was off to South America or somewhere to be a missionary.'

'Annie Stouton! Is it really? I can't believe it's you!'

'It's Annie Browne now, mum, and I've had another three since that first little girl, though the last one's not long since died. What are you doing back here then, mum?'

'Well I'm back in England for good now, Annie. Listen, do you have time to join me for a cup of tea? Is there a café nearby where we can go? I'd love to hear how things have been for you?' The wind was chilly and it had just begun spitting with rain. Annie looked around her, clearly unsure about whether she should leave her post.

'Well just a quick one can't hurt, can it? I've been here for a few hours already and I'm a bit frozen.'

She led the way to a small café on the street corner and we found a table near the window. I insisted we both have tea and toast and when I pretended I couldn't finish mine and pushed it across the table to her, she couldn't accept it quickly enough. In between mouthfuls she told me about her life which was clearly a struggle. Now married to Sid, a factory worker, she'd had three more babies in quick succession. They lived with her mother in a damp basement flat; her own father having walked out on them all years ago.

'So, what is this all about Annie?' I asked pointing to the bundle of leaflets. 'How on earth do you have the time to give out leaflets? Who is taking care of your children and more to the point what does all this "Votes for Women" stuff mean?'

'You needn't worry, my mum looks after the kids while I do this. But surely you've heard about the suffragette movement and Mrs Pankhurst, the lady what started it all?'

'Well I suppose so, but living in Peru all these years, I'm afraid to say I have been quite out of touch with things going on back in England. How did you become involved with it?'

So she explained. She told me about the Women's Social and Political Union, and how impressed she had been when almost by accident she'd attended a meeting, after what was called Black Friday in November 1910, when the Conciliation Bill to allow women the right to vote was dropped by parliament. A delegation of around 300 women suffragettes had staged a protest and many were assaulted, manhandled and arrested when they attempted to get past the lines of police.

'I'm sorry if I'm being a bit stupid, Annie, but I don't quite understand why women want the vote. Surely men with all their talk and trickery are the best suited to make the laws of the country, aren't they?'

'But don't you want to have a say in how the things that matter to you are run? Do you think it's fair that women don't have the same rights as men and that they get paid less than men for doing the same work? Even them rich women as own houses or pay taxes have no say in what those taxes should be spent on?'

I felt so foolish. Here was I, an educated woman, being told such an obvious truth by a poor working-class girl who, despite all my travels, was far more worldly-wise than me.

When we parted, I gave her a hug and insisted that I take her remaining leaflets, promising to distribute them to people on my way home. I showed the leaflet to Mac, even though I already knew what his reaction would be.

'I think it's a lot of nonsense, Beatrice. Why these women need to get so excited about something which they have done without all these years is quite beyond me. Personally, I think what *we* are doing, bringing God's Word to all those who live in darkness, is a bit more important.'

I wondered if becoming involved with the Women's Movement would help me feel part of something again so I spoke to Susannah about my meeting with Annie.

'Oh goodness Bea, how on earth would you find the time? You know what it's like with having a child to care for, a house to keep, clothes to be mended, food to buy and the whole place to keep clean. I don't have time to read the newspapers or go to meetings or have any sort of opinion about how the country is run. I don't have a spare minute in my day to even think about it. Wouldn't you rather leave such things to men?'

'But that is exactly what the problem is. Because men are the ones in charge, they can make laws to suit themselves and their male point of view. Women are different to men and so women require direct representation.'

'Well I suppose you have a point,' she replied as she put little Beatrice in her highchair.

'But Susannah, I need to find something worthwhile to do. I'll go mad if I have stay at home all day, and besides, what Annie was saying to me really made sense,' I said, aware of how emotional I was becoming. 'It was exactly the same in Peru. Women are exploited by the very people who should be upholding their rights; both priests and gentry. It isn't so bad for educated women who probably do have some influence, but what about Annie who has three children, lives in a damp basement and hardly has enough money to feed and clothe her family? She needs someone to act on her behalf.'

I realized that Susannah was not really listening as she bustled around setting the table for their supper and I left, wondering where I could meet other women locally who might be more amenable to discussion. But before I had an opportunity, my life changed once more.

One morning, a couple of weeks after meeting Annie Stouton, there was a slight chill in the air and a thin mist hung over the river. The trees were beginning to change into their autumn colours – I'd forgotten how the seasons changed in England and how much I used to love this time of year. I was eager to be outside and take a walk along the tow path. But after breakfast I felt rather sick and wondered if the fish I'd cooked the previous evening might have been bad, though Peggy and Mac seemed to be all right. When the same thing happened the next day and the next and I did a quick calculation in my head. Of course, how could I not have realized? I was pregnant! The part of me that was still angry with Mac had submitted to love making with little enthusiasm. It had been out of pure duty. But now that I was actually pregnant I was pleased and terrified in equal measure. As soon as I told Mac he insisted that I see a doctor immediately to check that everything was in order and for the next few months he fussed and chivvied and insisted that I do as little as possible. Every night he prayed on his knees that God would give us a healthy boy. He wanted to call the baby "John" as he assumed that since he wanted a son, he would have a son. So, when Jean was born on May 21st 1912, I tried to pacify him with the only girl's name I could think of that sounded like John.

CHAPTER 16

London 1912-1919

I was so preoccupied with caring for Jean as well as Peggy that, I'm ashamed to say, I completely forgot about Annie Stouton and the Women's Suffrage movement. The few leaflets I had taken from her remained in the kitchen drawer. It didn't help that no sooner had I begun to feel settled in Twickenham that we had to move again. The people who had rented us their house returned sooner than expected, and we moved to Palmers Green in North London to a house belonging to a colleague of Mac's. It was most unsettling. I no longer had Susannah just a few streets away and the few friendships I had made while in Twickenham didn't seem strong enough to withstand the move. At least we hadn't accumulated much and this time I could make sure that nothing was left behind; my precious mementoes were safe in the wooden chest.

Throughout the remainder of 1912, newspapers carried reports of women becoming even more militant in their cause for the vote. Prime Minister Asquith had his carriage attacked and in the centre of London, numerous pillar boxes had acid, ink, lampblack or tar poured into them, destroying thousands of letters.

'It's quite ridiculous,' scoffed Mac, who was back at home after a few weeks away on a lecture tour of the West Country. 'The Government will never do anything for these silly suffragette women as long as they behave as they do. They are unwomanly and ungodly and I fervently hope you are not going to get caught up with them.'

'Oh Mac, I've barely got the time to look after you, two children and the house, so I'm unlikely to be chaining myself to the railings outside Parliament,' I replied. 'And besides if I want to become involved, it will be as a *suffragist* not a suffragette.'

'It's all words to me,' he said.

'No, suffragists believe in peaceful protest using petitions and leaflets. I do think I could have a part to play helping them. I need to have a purpose, Mac. I don't want to be just a housewife and mother.'

'Beatrice, my dear, if you really have got the time to give out leaflets, I'd much rather you gave out leaflets for our missions in South America, whose need is somewhat greater, I believe.'

And that was the end of any discussion. Whatever I did he was probably going to think I was being disloyal. What was happening to us? We'd had our ups and downs like any normal couple while we were in Cuzco but when did we start nipping each other like a pair of unruly terriers?

Sadly, it was tragic news that brought us back together. At the end of December, we had a brief letter from Tom saying that Lily, the love of his life, had died very suddenly of typhoid. We were both devastated.

'Why, Mac, why? It is so unfair. Why should a couple like Tom and Lily, so devoted to God's work have to suffer so much? Why are all the people I love taken from me? Why is God so mean? And please don't tell me to think about Christ's suffering on the cross.'

'I know Beatrice, it's hard. I wish I had an answer to give you.' Just for once, he didn't utter his usual platitude about God working in mysterious ways. Instead, he put his arms around me until I stopped crying. I felt so sad but also grateful and relieved that we could still reach out to one another. I looked into his eyes and all I could see was an intense weariness. I felt guilty because I had become so wrapped up in my own issues I hadn't noticed how exhausted he had become with his endless lecture tours, meetings and introductory letters he'd insisted on writing to all the missionaries now under the EUSA umbrella.

So, I never did become any more involved with the Suffragette movement. What spare time I had, I devoted to helping Mac with his letters and articles. Who could say which cause was the more important – "Votes for Women" or votes for God? I didn't really want to have to make the choice. But as I read in the newspapers that more and more women were being imprisoned and force fed when they refused to eat, I was actually quite glad that I hadn't become involved. And when Emily Davison, the suffragette, who ran out in front of the King's horse at the Epsom Derby in June 1913 was trampled to death, I began to agree with Mac, that things had gone quite far enough. Surely women gaining the vote, important though it was, was not worth dying for?

But then came those dreadful years of war when millions

of lives were lost or destroyed. In my memory, those years were always dark and cold. Everything smelt of dampness or charred rubber.

To begin with, like everyone else, we believed that it would all be over by Christmas and our day-to-day life continued much as before. In the autumn of 1914 the directors of EUSA became very concerned about a serious problem that had arisen concerning the missionaries in Brazil and they asked Mac to go over in person and sort it out. He was very pleased to be returning to South America, but because of the uncertainty of the war, his trip kept getting delayed. Eventually it was decided that the problems in Brazil could wait no longer and he set sail from Liverpool on April 12th 1915. Every day I waited for news of his safe arrival. Every day I imagined his ship being sunk by a German submarine. Even if he reached Brazil safely, how long would it take for a letter from him to come back? I was terribly worried and my efforts to hide this from the children failed abysmally. On the evening of May 7th after I heard the news that the *Lusitania* had been sunk all three of us curled up together for comfort in my bed. When, two days later, a brief letter from Mac arrived we cried and laughed and hugged each other.

But the relief was short-lived. On May 31st, ten days after Jean's third birthday, one of the first Zeppelin raids struck Stoke Newington, not far from where we lived. It was such a shock. I never imagined that what was happening in France and Belgium would spread as far as England. How could ordinary people be attacked in their homes? Weren't wars supposed to be fought by men on battlefields? The following day, I left the children with a neighbour and went to inspect the damage for myself. Beside the smoking rubble, small groups of people huddled together, looking quite dazed. From time to time they looked skywards as if they could still see the airship that had caused such destruction. No one had ever experienced anything like it. After all, there hadn't been a war or a battle on English soil for centuries. But as the raids by the so-called "baby-killers" continued, I began to feel quite lonely. Susannah had problems of her own; her husband's grocery business had failed just before the war and she had to take on several part-time jobs to make ends meet. I saw Sidney and Millie from time to time but everyone always seemed to be busy.

Jean was far too young to understand what was happening; for her, cocoa and stories by torchlight under the stairs became quite an adventure. But Peggy was very worried about her father and terrified when the raids occurred. I kept telling them that their father would be home soon but as the weeks passed with no more letters from him, once more I felt abandoned. I also felt rather embarrassed trying to explain to people where he was and why he wasn't involved in some sort of war effort in England. To make up for his absence I did what I could, though knitting or darning socks seemed rather pathetic.

Every week I wrote a long letter to him filled with trivia about what I or the girls had been doing. Somehow, I assumed he would receive general news about the war but to spare him any worry I omitted details about bombs, ruined buildings or the alarming rise of wounded or dead soldiers. Gradually a small trickle of letters from Mac did arrive but they contained only the barest details of what he was doing and since each letter had been written weeks before, I still had no sense of where he actually was.

Every week I asked the directors at EUSA when he would be coming home. Bizarrely they seemed to take the attitude that their war against poverty, ignorance and the corruption of Catholic church, was just as important as what was happening here and in Europe. How they could ignore the numbers of men being killed or wounded day after day was quite beyond me. And then, to make matters worse, because of the danger from German U-boats to shipping crossing the Atlantic, they suggested he extend his trip to include visits to Argentina and Peru. I imagined that they thought I was making a fuss about nothing. When at last Mac wrote to me from Peru, although he claimed that he was missing us all, reading between the lines, I could tell that he was quite delighted to be back in his beloved Cuzco.

Just before my birthday in November I received a much longer letter.

"Dearest Beatrice, I have such exciting news. Do you remember the evening when that American explorer, Hiram Bingham came to dinner with us at Monjaspata, and I mentioned the Inca ruins which poor old Franklin had described? At the time we thought no more about it but it seems that Professor Bingham came back to Cuzco not long after we'd left and he discovered the ruins for himself. Tom showed me a 1913 issue of the National Geographic magazine in which Bingham claimed to have discovered the ruins at a place called Machu Picchu, exactly where Franklin had said they would be. I was quite annoyed that nowhere in the article did he mention either me or Franklin as being the ones who tipped him off, nor the fact

that there was an Indian family actually living and farming amongst the ruins when he first came across them

But now I have finally seen them for myself. Bingham has just completed some extensive excavations and returned to America, but Tom and I persuaded one of his local guides to take us and what an experience that was! The climb was something I shall never forget. Up the sheer face of the two thousand feet cliff, by fragments of a trail left by the Indians, clinging to cracks and crevices, we made our painful way until we stood at last at the point where we could see the partly cleared ruins below us. There was a broad staircase of roughly hewn stone which led to the city gate, where, in the great jambs of beautifully cut stone, we saw lock-holes cut in the stone. We could also see a little column of stone, round which the cables were made fast that held the gate beams in position. But what really excited me were the three windows. Remember that according to legend, Manco Capac and his three brothers are supposed to have emerged from three windows. And there they were – three enormous windows with such perfection of stone cutting that I've never seen before. It was all so magnificent.

Just imagine, Beatrice, if we had yielded to old Franklin's entreaties to go and explore the ruins for ourselves, we should have been, to adapt Coleridge – "The first that ever burst into that silent scene." I do so wish that you could have been there with me, Beatrice."

So perhaps he was beginning to miss me after all. Although at the time, I thought how bizarre it was, that Mac was so enthralled by ancient Inca ruins, while all over London, almost on our own doorstep, new ruins were being created every day.

He finally returned in March 1916 and was very shocked by what he came home to. He'd heard and read practically nothing of the war while he'd been away. It was if he'd been in another world. Although he was safely over the age limit for conscription it was agreed that he would adopt the title of Reverend, which would guarantee his exemption even if they did raise the age. Peggy was thrilled to have her father home again and treated him as if he was a wounded soldier home from the trenches, following him from room to room, making him cups of tea and plumping the cushion on his chair. Jean didn't seem to recognise him at all and for quite a while, much to his annoyance, she rejected his attempts at affection towards her. But at last we were a family again.

For the remainder of the war we both did whatever we could to help families from our church who had lost husbands and fathers. Although Mac still had his responsibilities for the missions in South America, he also spent many hours visiting wounded soldiers in hospitals in London. I belonged to several women's groups involved with raising funds, making and mending clothes, and sorting out items to donate to soldiers for Christmas.

The war seemed to go on and on. Relentless. Everybody was exhausted when peace finally came. But no sooner had the Armistice been signed, there was the awful influenza epidemic. Surprisingly it was mostly young babies and healthy grownups who were attacked. But gradually as it spread, hundreds of poor soldiers, who'd somehow survived the terror of the trenches, were wiped out by it as soon as they returned home. There was a lovely family who lived next door to us. Rose, the mother, was quite a bit younger than me and she had three little ones, all under the age of seven. We'd helped each other out all the time during the war and had such fun decorating her house with streamers for when Bill, her husband, returned from France. He'd only been home for a week, when early one morning, Rose knocked at our door and asked Mac to take a look at Bill, who'd been shivering all night with a fever. I'll never forget the sight of him that morning. His skin was a vivid purple – a definite sign of the flu. I insisted that her children must be kept away from him and that I'd look after them until he was better. But he died that same day and two days later Rose went too. Those poor children. They stayed with us for a week or so until their grandmother arrived to take them in. I don't know what became of them. I never heard from the family ever again. It really affected me. Would all this suffering never stop? Whose turn would it be next?

By the time it was all over – both the war and the influenza – there was hardly anyone who hadn't lost a loved one. Quite dreadful. It was all such a ridiculous waste of life. And so while Mac's faith in the Almighty grew stronger, mine become flimsy and threadbare. I still went to church and took part in our family evening prayers and bible reading but to be honest, my heart simply wasn't in it anymore.

CHAPTER 17

London and Edinburgh 1919-1923

For a while it was as though everything that had become familiar and safe had fallen apart. Friends lost, neighbours uprooted, lives ruined, my faith in tatters. I didn't know what I believed in anymore. Mac had always said that having doubts or a wavering faith was a necessary part of God's plan to prevent us from becoming self-satisfied or complacent. But a God who could allow the carnage of the war wasn't one I could understand or believe in.

So as I had done before, when my father, my two sisters and my brother Gordon all died within a few months of each other, I kept myself as busy as I could – anything that would block out my feelings. So much had changed as a result of the war. Although I hadn't done anything to help the suffragette cause, at least women like myself now had a vote (even if it was only because I was the wife of a householder). But women like poor Annie Stouton, for all her standing in the freezing cold distributing leaflets, still had no rights. I was determined to become properly involved in something which would benefit women.

It was a throw-away remark by my sister-in-law, Millie,

which gave me an idea. I recalled the fuss there had been towards the end of 1918 when a woman called Marie Stopes had published a book called "Married Love". It was the first book to suggest that marriage should be an equal relationship and that women too, had sexual desires. What made it such an instant success, as well as an endless controversy, was that it contained sensible advice about how to avoid unwanted pregnancies. (Not that Mac or I needed any advice; our sex life, such as it was, had ground to a halt shortly after Jean was born.) Having witnessed the distress of so many women both in the East End of London and in Cuzco, when repeated pregnancies ruined their health and plunged them deeper into poverty with yet another mouth to feed, the concept that women could now be in charge was good news indeed. I thought of my own mother and I was sure that she might have lived much longer if she hadn't had so many exhausting pregnancies. I tried to discuss the ideas with Mac, but he, like so many others, thought that Stopes was promoting abortion and killing innocent babies, rather than ensuring that every baby would be planned and wanted.

One afternoon, without telling Mac, I took the train into central London to hear Marie Stopes giving a lecture. From the moment she started speaking, I was captivated. She was an attractive woman, quite pale, but with deep brown eyes and a mass of dark hair piled up on her head. She was clearly well-educated and spoke most eloquently. At one moment, she stopped to sip from a glass of water and I learnt from the woman sitting next to me that Marie Stopes had recently lost her first baby, stillborn after a very traumatic full-term delivery. I knew exactly how she must feel, and yet, here she was, desperate for her own child, telling others how to avoid pregnancy. I was sitting near the front and she must have seen me nodding my head in agreement because each time she looked towards me she smiled. When she had finished speaking I introduced myself, sympathised with her loss and asked what I could do to help. We spoke for some while and she gave me some leaflets as well as a copy of her book, *Wise Parenthood*, and told me to go out and spread the word. The irony of Mac handing out pamphlets about the word of God and me handing out pamphlets about the words of Marie Stopes was not lost on me.

For a while, my days became quite hectic; getting the children off to school, washing, cleaning, ironing, sewing and mending, shopping, preparing meals and, whenever I could, travelling to the East End to distribute leaflets and talk to women's groups. I felt inspired. Once again, I had a purpose and I was involved in something which was important and worthwhile. Marie Stopes even asked me personally to be on the committee planning the opening of a "Mother's Clinic" in Holloway. The clinic would be run by midwives and supported by visiting doctors. Any women who attended would be taught a variety of methods of contraception.

Since Mac didn't approve and kept reminding me that I was neglecting our missionary work, I rarely mentioned my new interest. He was also very busy travelling around the country making speeches and fundraising. But increasingly he would return home, quite irritable and dejected, because since the war, people had become less willing to donate money for missions overseas, when there was so much need here, on their own doorsteps.

Things came to a head one rainy weekend in October. It was nearly Jean's bedtime and I was in the kitchen with Peggy, working through a pile of mending when Jean ran into the room in tears.

'What on earth is the matter?' I asked as I wrapped her in my arms.

'It's Father. He's destroyed all my picture cards,' she sobbed. She had decided to show him her collection of picture cards which came in packets of cigarettes. My brother, Walter, used to save them for her. Her favourite collection was of different wild animals. She'd been so excited to show Mac her full set. But with a grim silence, he had taken each card, examined it, and slowly dunked it into his cup of tea before tossing the soggy remains into the waste bin. I was furious. I comforted Jean as best I could and then asked Peggy, to take her upstairs and help her get ready for bed, while I talked to their father.

I strode into the front room where Mac was sitting on the sofa, reading a newspaper.

'How could you do that to Jeanie? What on earth were you thinking of?'

He looked at me over the top of the newspaper. 'She needs to understand that smoking cigarettes is a filthy, disgusting, evil habit.'

'Oh, for goodness sake, Mac, the child is only eight years old. She isn't interested in smoking, she simply likes the pictures and she has been waiting for weeks to show you her full collection.'

He made no reply. Why did he have to be so obstinate and unreasonable? I was about to leave the room when to my surprise, he covered his face with his hands and burst into tears. And as he wept he rocked, forward and back.

Quickly I closed the door and sat down beside him.

'I'm sorry that I've upset Jeanie, but I can't do this anymore. I simply can't do it,' he sobbed.

'What is it that you can't do anymore?' I asked softly.

'All of it.'

I put my arms around him and held him close to me. Slowly his sobs subsided.

I thought back over the past few months. At last, I'd begun to feel more settled and fulfilled with all the things I'd taken on. So, I suppose I hadn't taken much notice of Mac's gradually changing mood. To be truthful I had learnt to ignore his quick temper, his frustration with the children, his rants about the trustees of EUSA, and his sullen silences at meal times. 'This is just how he is,' I'd told myself.

But now as I stroked his hair, I felt an old flare of love for him. Slowly he sat up and blew his nose.

'I just feel so awful. It's like being in a dark place, alone and abandoned and trapped. Every day I pray that it will pass and I will feel whole again, but it's always the same. I don't think God is listening to me. Everything I do seems pointless and any goodness I might have had once has been sucked out of me by the Devil.'

He fell silent for a while. I didn't know what to say to him. I had no idea that he felt like this. He'd never shown any vulnerability or weakness. Men just didn't.

'I don't know what I'm doing any more, Beatrice,' he continued. 'The passion for what I was doing in Cuzco seems to have vanished. I was happy out there. We both were. But now it's all so far away. I no longer feel part of it.

I don't belong anywhere. No one seems to need me – the missionaries out in in the field do whatever they want, I haven't heard from Tom in ages, and even the congregations I speak to on my lecture tours seem to have lost interest. What is the point of it all?' He blew his nose again and looked at me.

'And, you Beatrice, I watch everything you do; for the children, for your family, for our church, for your wretched pregnant women, and you have a good reason to get out of bed each day. What do I get up for, tell me that?' He began to cry again.

'How long have you been feeling like this?'

'It feels like forever but I suppose it's only been these past nine months or so.'

'Oh dear Mac, for so long? I'm so sorry. How could I not have noticed? Why didn't you say anything?' I held his hand and he squeezed mine back.

'It's all my fault, Beatrice. I should have listened to you. I think I made a big mistake bringing us back from Cuzco, but at the time I really did believe that it was the right decision. But now I am beginning to wish that there was some way we could all go back.'

I was shocked. Part of me felt a flutter of excitement at the idea of returning to our proper home at Monjaspata, but a much bigger part thought, 'No! I am not uprooting our family and dragging the girls halfway round the world. It wouldn't be fair or even sensible.'

'No Mac. I'm sorry,' I said firmly. 'It's much too late. We can't go back. I think I understand how hard things are for you right now, but there has to be another way to help you feel better.'

It was now past nine. I realised I hadn't checked on the girls and hoped that Peggy had put Jean to bed. It was enough for one day. Mac looked exhausted and I felt drained.

The following day, Mac was able to apologise to Jeanie and although he was relieved to have told me how depressed he was, he clearly wasn't in a fit state to do any work. Reluctantly he cancelled a lecture tour of the Midlands and the Trustees accepted that he needed to take some time off work. I stopped everything I was doing on behalf of Marie Stopes and told her that I could no longer spare the time for the opening of the clinic. Every day, I found a good reason for Mac to get dressed and leave the house for a while, either on an errand or on a walk with me, or meeting the children from school.

One evening, some weeks later, after we had taken tea with Sidney and Millie, he asked me to accompany him to Edinburgh for a few days to visit his brother, George, whom he had not seen for a long while. I had kept in touch with all my siblings over the years; I loved both writing and receiving their letters and hearing all the news. But Mac had pretty much lost touch with all his family, including George, who had been instrumental in his conversion.

'I feel so guilty for neglecting them, they deserved more. I kept meaning to write but somehow other things seemed more important,' he said sadly. 'I watch you with your brothers and sisters and there is so much warmth between you all. I don't remember ever having that sense of belonging with mine. I think it might do me good if I could talk to George about my work and the difficulties I am having with it. I'm sure he still lives at the same place and perhaps it's not too late mend the bridge between us.' He paused and seized my hand. 'But it would be a big help if you came along with me.'

'Of course I'll come, if you really want me to, but what about the girls?'

'It only needs to be for a couple of days. Couldn't you ask Sidney or Susannah if the girls could stay with them? Please!'

And so I made all the arrangements and we went. As the train pulled into Edinburgh Waverly station, Mac looked more cheerful than I had seen him in months. I had never been to Edinburgh and had always imagined it to be rather cold and windy. But it was a warm sunny day. The castle looked magnificent and the wide streets of elegant houses in Princes Street and St Andrew's Square were such a contrast to our somewhat seedy road in Palmers Green.

George was pleased to see us, but he was clearly a sick man. His wife had died some years ago and having no children he was being cared for by a housekeeper who popped in each day. Two heart attacks had left him very thin with pallid skin, swollen ankles and an awful cough which made him breathless and exhausted. In between coughing fits, he shared shreds of family news and listened intently while we told him about our life and work in Peru. So that we didn't overtire him, Mac showed me all the sights of Edinburgh. We looked down over the town from Arthur's Seat, or "My Seat" as Mac fondly called it, his first name being Arthur. He showed me the house in Hart Street where he had grown up and we visited the church where the stained glass window he'd designed glowed brightly as the sun streamed through it. It was beautiful.

The days we spent in Edinburgh were wonderful. We smiled and laughed and enjoyed each other. Mac looked renewed and alive in a way that I had missed for so long. While he'd been so depressed it was like living with ghost; he was there but out of reach. Nothing I did or said made any difference. It was worse than the times when we argued and when the hole between us seemed too big to mend. It was such a relief to feel close with him again. On the train as we returned to London, Mac said,

'Beatrice, I know this a lot to ask of you, but I would dearly love us all to move back here to Edinburgh. I hadn't realised how much I had missed it and coming back has felt like coming home. Now that I have been reunited with George I need to be near him and do whatever I can for him in the time he has left.' He paused and looked out of the window as the Scottish lowlands flashed by. 'And besides, we have both been so happy in these past few days; I think it would be good for us both. I'm sure the children would love to get away from London and breathe some clean Scottish air.'

Once again, I gave in to what Mac wanted, and in the autumn of 1921 I uprooted the girls and we moved to Edinburgh.

I was sad to miss the opening of Marie Stopes' very first birth control clinic and disappointed that nearly all the strict Scottish Presbyterians I met, profoundly disapproved of her revolutionary ideas about family planning. Consequently, I spent my days trying to make the small, cold, dingy house we rented feel like a pleasant, cosy family home. We visited George most days and it was clear that he was grateful for our care and concern. The girls attended the Edinburgh Ladies College, a good local school which was recommended by a woman who attended George's church. I knew they didn't like it at first, but I dismissed most of their complaints as it just taking a while for them to settle in to such a new environment.

I accompanied Mac whenever he gave talks and lectures and I wrote endless letters to a variety of organisations to raise funds for EUSA. I think Mac was pleased that he had at last reigned me in. I missed my friends and family in London dreadfully but Mac insisted that it would be good for all of us to experience a different sort of culture and become adept at making new friends. Gradually I got used to the cold windy days and the rain. To begin with, Mac seemed to thrive. He made fairly frequent trips to London for meetings of the trustees at the central EUSA office and once or twice I went with him and met up with my family.

Several months after we'd moved to Edinburgh, his brother, George, died. Mac was distraught and I feared that he would relapse into another depression. He had been so much better since we'd left London. And towards the end of '22, what I had dreaded happened again. Mac did become depressed. Apart from his brother's death I wasn't sure what else might have triggered the episode and this time he became even more monosyllabic and withdrawn. When he did speak, he complained about everything; the house was too untidy; the meals I cooked were too bland; the girls were too noisy; people at our church were bad-mouthing him. I began to dread every meal time and as soon as they were excused Peggy and Jean disappeared upstairs to their bedroom, leaving me to try and encourage Mac into a better mood.

The Trustees were well aware of the problems and once again decided it was time for Mac to pay another visit to the missionary groups in Peru, Argentina and Brazil. After all, it had been six years since his last trip. The change in Mac was almost instantaneous and I was relieved that at last we would all have a break from him. But one evening he said,

'I want you to come with me this time, Beatrice.'

'Don't be ridiculous, I can't possibly leave the girls.'

'Please, Beatrice. I need you by my side. It wouldn't be for very long and I am sure we could find a family from church who would be willing to look after the girls. Surely they are quite old enough to cope with us going away for a short while. You are far too soft with them. I spent almost my whole childhood without a mother and you're objecting to leaving them for a couple of months.'

'I don't think that would be at all fair Mac, neither for the children or some family they don't know. No, it's quite out of the question.'

'You might spare a thought, Beatrice, for all the missionaries out there in South America. Is it fair to leave them to cope with doing the Lord's work with no support from the organisation that sent them out there?'

'But you'll be visiting them, they don't need both of us, do they?'

I thought that would be the end of it, but every day he persisted. He pointed out that plenty of parents worked abroad, sent their children to boarding school and only saw them once or twice a year in the holidays.

'And besides, Beatrice, wouldn't you love to see our beloved Monjaspata again and Tom and all our good friends who are still out there?'

'Well, it would be lovely. But couldn't we wait and take the girls with us in the long holiday?'

'No. Beatrice, it would be far too expensive for us all to go and anyway this will be a trip for work, not some jolly holiday. The Trustees will pay my fare and they might be willing to make a contribution for yours.'

I was so tempted. I yearned to see how my garden had fared over the years and it would be so good to spend some time with Tom, and perhaps see Sophia, all grown up.

And so, I agreed. I ignored the voice in my head that questioned how I could leave my children with strangers. I banished the memory of their distraught faces when we told them the news. And I reassured myself that the McGoverns were a lovely family and that the girls would be well cared for in our absence.

CHAPTER 18

Peru 1923

What really helped me to make the decision was the thought that, just for once, I was going to do something for myself; something that wasn't about duty or pleasing anyone else, or even doing it for Mac. Just for once I would do something for me.

On April 26th 1923 we set sail from Liverpool on *SS Orya* bound for Lima. The voyage was so much shorter because this time we went through the Panama Canal. I can't believe I was so naïve; I'd somehow imagined that the Panama Canal would be something similar to the canals and locks of the Thames, on a slightly larger scale! I was quite unprepared for the eleven or so hours it took the ship to make its slow progress from east to west. The whole voyage was wonderful; there was nothing I needed to do; no one clamoured for my attention; I could sit and stare at the waves for as long as I liked and I would not allow any guilty feelings about the girls. For the first time in a long while, I felt free. Mac and I talked and laughed and enjoyed being with each other, just as we had when we first made the voyage over there, nineteen years ago.

As before, we spent a night in Lima before journeying on to Mollendo and Arequipa. Flo and John Jarrett were no longer in Peru, having moved to Columbia just after the war, and in a way, I was glad that we could press on to Cuzco. I was very excited as I gazed out of the train window, drinking in all the scenery I had missed for so long.

When the train arrived in the early evening at Cuzco, there was the usual rush of Indian boys into the carriage to secure the baggage, and on the platform we were greeted by a tall, thin man who introduced himself as Rev. Milham. Standing beside him, quite unchanged, was dear Ethel Pinn. She beamed at me, hugged me tightly and then linking her arm with mine led us through the crowd and up the hill to Monjaspata. Mac and the Rev. Milham followed and checked that the boys were bringing our bags. I'd completely forgotten about the effect the altitude would have on me and the breathlessness I'd felt on the train returned once more as we walked. Both Mac and I had to stop several times in the dimly lit street to catch our breath.

'I don't want you to be too shocked,' said Ethel while I was resting for a moment, 'but you need to know that there have been a few changes to the Monjaspata which you knew and loved.'

'I expect lots of things have changed,' I panted, 'but I imagine that wonderful view from the balcony will still be the same.'

From the outside, our house (I still felt it was ours), was not much changed in itself, but it was now surrounded by several other buildings: a small six bedded hospital, a dispensary, a small chapel and a school. Every room in the house was full, with two nurses, a doctor and his family, as well as Rev. Milham and a teacher. Somehow, they had all contrived to double up so that Sophia's old room was available for Mac and me to sleep in. We were exhausted with both the travelling and the altitude and after a welcoming supper of *Chupee* stew, we both retired to our room, sleepy but contented.

The following morning, I woke very early before anyone else was up. I slipped out of bed, leaving Mac asleep and tip-toed into the garden. There were quite a few flowers around the edges of the garden and most of the land had been given over to vegetables. But my bench was still there, framed by bougainvillea blossom and I sat down to take it all in. It was cool and I wrapped my alpaca shawl around my shoulders. The wool no longer smelt of babies; it had been safely folded away when Jeanie no longer needed it, but I'd been determined to bring it with me on the trip. I could have sat there all morning listening to the spring water as it trickled through the stone channel into our little stream, now crowded by ferns; water which had flowed from some mysterious underground source since Inca times. After a while, I became aware of sounds and voices coming from the kitchen and before anyone could interrupt me, I walked over to the stream to check that the stone which covered Baby Peter was still in place. He would have been a big lad of nearly fourteen, if he'd lived. It was still there. It hadn't been moved although it was hidden by ferns and covered with pale green moss. Thank goodness, he was still safe and undisturbed. Quickly I scattered some bougainvillea petals over the stone and returned to the house.

By the time Mac woke up, everyone was already at work and after some breakfast we stood on the little balcony to gaze at the panorama. It was exactly as I'd remembered; range after range of mountain-tops faded into the shining blue distance. And in the center, the single snow-topped mountain, standing like a sentinel, guarding the valley. I squeezed Mac's hand. England and the children seemed so far away and strangely, I didn't care, because at last I had come home.

For the first few days I did feel as if I had come home to somewhere that I truly belonged, because the years we lived there were the happiest years of our lives, despite losing Peter. But that feeling didn't last.

On the voyage over I had imagined that the nurses would be only too grateful for another pair of hands to help out both at Monjaspata and in Cuzco in the patient's houses. In some ways, it was as if we had never left, but then again, so much had changed over the ten years. My nursing and midwifery skills were apparently out-of-date and although everyone was very kind, they were also very busy and I think they saw me more as a visitor who required entertaining. And since I was no longer part of the work of the mission, I didn't really feel that I had a place there anymore. It was hard being a guest in what still felt like *my house*.

Mac was in his element. Whereas I had forgotten much of my Spanish and Quechua, he was able to ride out to some of the nearby villages and pay visits to some of his early converts, as well as being invited to preach at the evening meetings in the town. I knew he would have liked to stay longer.

It was lovely to meet up with Mrs Recharte again, and

young Sophia, who was now married, proudly introduced me to her own two children, though she was disappointed that we hadn't brought Peggy with us. And then there was Tom.

We stayed at Urco for over a week. I had been looking forward so much to seeing him again. Of course, he'd been in regular correspondence with Mac and it was wonderful to see all the changes he'd made. He'd rebuilt most of the original buildings using timber which he had ambitiously floated down the Vilcanota River on rafts, rather than using mules or donkeys which would have taken months. Mr and Mrs Job were still there and had established a flourishing school with tables and chairs made from old boxes and a proper blackboard with chalk. All the classes were held in the evenings when the Indians had finished work. It was still such a beautiful place; miles of terraces growing vegetables and orchards of cherry, quince, peach and olive.

On the evening we arrived, they made a wonderful feast for us, the labourers and their wives and children. There was a great copper cauldron full of a steaming hot *Chupee* stew of sheep and goat meat as well as buckets of potatoes, cabbage, onions and all sorts of things. Every scrap of food was eaten and afterwards Mac gave a magic lantern show. It was so good to see the delight on the faces of these solid looking people who rarely seem to smile. How they talked and laughed when an old fox from London Zoo appeared on the screen; one of the shepherds jumped up, saying in a most tragic voice: "Let us kill him for he eats our sheep."

But so much had happened to Tom since we had last seen him and it simply wasn't the same anymore. Not only was my dear friend Lily gone, but all traces of her having lived there had vanished. Alice, Tom's wife whom he had married in 1914, could not have been more different. I think Tom was quite anxious about what I would think of him marrying again, just barely two years after Lily's death. Alice was pleasant enough but deliberately vague when I asked what had happened to the lovely watercolours Lily had painted. But on the day we left, Tom led me to an untidy room which served as his office and pulled three small paintings of Lily's from a cupboard; a view of the mountains from the front door; a sprig of purple bougainvillea; a group of Indian women in bright skirts.

'I know Lily would have wanted you to have something of hers. Please take these, Beatrice, from both of us.'

'All of them, Tom? Are you sure you don't mind?'

'Not at all, dear Beatrice. Her paintings need to be seen, not tucked away.'

'Thank you so much. I promise that these three lovely watercolours will be hung on a wall wherever I live.'

Suddenly I felt much better about our trip. I had been so disappointed in Cuzco that so much had changed. Nothing had been quite as I'd imagined. I was afraid I'd lost all the threads that had connected me with Peru. But now, at least I would have a part of Tom and Lily with me for ever.

The whole purpose of the trip was to visit, not only Peru, but also all the missionaries in Argentina and Brazil. Mac had to visit every mission and ensure that EUSA funds were being spent appropriately. All this took longer than we expected because some of their problems took many hours of discussion to resolve. But Mac loved every minute; the missionaries were delighted to have someone from the central office spend time with them, praise their achievements, understand their difficulties and inspire them to continue with the work, however hard it was. And although I was as warmly welcomed as Mac, I had nothing to do and no role, other than being his wife.

At first I was quite envious of Mac but gradually I allowed myself to let go and enjoy what was the first proper holiday I'd ever had. We spent hours and hours on trains which gave me plenty of time to think. I missed my girls but I also enjoyed having no responsibilities. All my life had been taken up with looking after others; I had rarely spent time or energy looking after myself. Someone always wanted something from me. As I gazed out of the train window at the scenery rushing past, I felt exhausted. I realised that I didn't want to fight for any more causes. I'd done enough. It was someone else's turn and besides, what use was I to others if I was drained and empty myself?

I wondered about how I could fit some precious time, just for me, into the daily busyness of being a wife and mother. And if I did, how would I use it? I had no aspirations to become a writer or an artist which might be a valid excuse, so how would I explain it to Mac? I jotted down some ideas on the back of an envelope and then it came to me. I would keep a journal of some sort; not one that would catalogue all the petty comings and goings, but a private place where I could voice my thoughts, my dreams, my dilemmas – my purpose in life. And I would start right now. In the next town we came to, I bought a small notebook with a brightly coloured cover and a fountain pen. And I began to write.

After my disappointment with our visit to Peru, in the end, I found the whole trip really fascinating. Three countries, each so different; Peru with its vast mountain ranges were such a contrast to the flat plains of Argentina which stretched endlessly towards the horizon and beyond; and finally, the mysterious, green forests and jungles of Brazil.

Travelling around such a vast continent took forever. We were stranded for nearly a week in a small town in Argentina after a fierce storm brought all forms of transport to a complete halt. A whole day of rain in England was bad enough but I had never seen anything like the torrential downpour we were caught up in. Fortunately, we were staying in a two-storey house, since the street below had become a deep muddy river and there was nothing we could do until the water subsided enough for us to get a rowing boat ride to the station and wait for a train.

But as we travelled towards Buenos Aires, on a track which was just above the water level, we saw similar conditions. The desolation in the single-storey houses must have been dreadful and how people were existing with anything between three and six feet of water flowing through their rooms was a mystery. Rows of wretched bedraggled chickens sat along the fence tops; shivering horses stood knee deep in water on the highest ground they could reach; debris of all kinds floated everywhere. Such a sad, wet wilderness.

Brazil was a complete contrast. We travelled for miles and miles through forested hills and fields of green-leafed coffee bushes planted in crimson red soil. On one of the journeys, about forty miles from our destination, the train broke down on a steep incline. Amid a tremendous clanking and roar of escaping steam, the train started back downhill. It was quite alarming until at last the brakes brought us to a standstill. It was early evening and we all had to get off the train and sit on the embankment while the engine was repaired. Everyone was quite cheerful and philosophical about the breakdown and we witnessed the most spectacular sunset which we might otherwise have missed. Eventually the train driver, bizarrely wearing an immaculate white waistcoat and yellow shoes, managed to repair the engine sufficiently to make it up the hill and then down again to the next station where we waited through the night for a replacement train.

Delays of this sort were quite commonplace but it meant that we missed the ship we were due to sail home on. So, the trip which was only supposed to last for a couple of months took much longer. No wonder the girls were so upset.

Edinburgh 1923

When we finally arrived back at Edinburgh Waverley station the girls were waiting for us on the platform. I was shocked by how they looked. They were both pale and although Jean had grown taller, they both looked thinner. Instead of whoops of pleasure at seeing us, they burst into tears. Peggy gave Mac an awkward hug but Jean clung to me as if she'd never let me go. It was if we had been away for years, not nine months.

Our house, left empty while we'd been away, smelt damp and unfriendly but it still felt good to be home again. It was

November and quite chilly so while Mac got a fire going I went to the corner shop to buy some food for supper.

'It's been really awful, Mother, why did you leave us for so long with those terrible people?' blurted Peggy as she helped me peel some potatoes. 'The McGoverns were really horrible to us.'

'Oh, surely not Peggy. What on earth do you mean?'

'There were lots of things. If Jeanie ever said she didn't like one of the over-boiled vegetables we were meant to eat, Mrs McGovern would say, "*Och, the troubles that beset us and the trials we endure!*" with a stupid smile on her face and she'd whip the whole plate away and give her nothing else. And once, when I was doubled up with a period pain she dragged me off my bed, pushed me out of the front door and told me that if Jesus could endure pain, then so could I.'

I didn't know what to say. The McGoverns had seemed quite happy to have the children come to stay with them, though naturally they hadn't expected it to be for as long as it was. I felt so guilty. I put my arms around her, 'I'm so sorry my love. I had no idea it would turn out like this. But we are home now. We are all together and I won't ever leave you again.'

I had imagined our first meal together being full of smiles and laughter as Mac and I told the girls all about our adventures. Instead we became more and more subdued as they explained how hard it had been for them.

'And at school, they were horrid to us as well,' said Jean. They called Peggy, "the girl in the green jumper" and they called me "the sister of the girl in the green jumper" and they said we talked posh and pretended to talk like us, but anyway we couldn't understand their accents, and Miss MacNally made me stand in the corner when I got my sums wrong, and why didn't you bring me back the parrot that you promised me?' she finished breathlessly.

'Oh sweetheart, I am so sorry. We did look for a parrot but we didn't think it would survive the voyage home. Come on girls, let's get you both to bed. It's been quite a day.'

For the rest of the evening I felt dreadful. The voice in my head asked me how I could have been so selfish and let my children down so badly? See what happens when you shirk your duties and just please yourself? Don't you think you've made a bit of a mess of things, both as a mother and as a wife?

But how could I have got it right? I argued back. Mac insisted that I went with him. And besides, if we hadn't both gone to South America, it's likely that his depression and our marriage might have been in an even worse state, I retorted.

Well, perhaps if you hadn't been so busy and wrapped up in all those so-called worthy causes and activities Mac wouldn't have become depressed in the first place.

And so on, back and forth the argument raged in my head.

'Come to bed, Beatrice,' said Mac when he came downstairs after unpacking the suitcases and found me sitting in the dark. 'We'll all feel better after we've had a good night's sleep.'

He was as upset as I by what the girls had told us and he acknowledged that living in Scotland had been a mistake. As soon as he could, he made all the necessary arrangements and in the spring of 1924 we moved back to London. It was the first house move I had ever looked forward to.

London 1924-1939

For the next few years we lived in a small house in West Norwood and I was determined to put all my energy into being a good wife and mother; keeping house, helping Mac, and making sure that Jean and Peggy got as much of my attention as they needed. It was such a relief to see the girls happy again and actually enjoy going to school.

And most days, despite the annoying voice in my head, I sat in an armchair with a view of the back garden and I wrote in my journal.

But inevitably, in 1928 we were on the move again! Mr Ervine, who was then the chairman of the EUSA board, generously donated his large house in Denmark Hill to the mission and that is where we lived right up until the start of the war. We had use of the spacious rooms upstairs, while the day-to-day work of the mission continued on the ground floor.

But it seemed that no sooner had we moved to a house with much more space, that it quickly became empty. Peggy was the first to leave when she went to train to be a nanny at the esteemed Norland College. She had always been good with children and her heart was set on becoming a missionary herself. And a couple of years later Jean won a place to study medicine at the Royal Free Hospital in Hampstead – the only teaching hospital to admit women for medical training. Mac couldn't understand why she didn't train to be a nurse like other girls, but I knew she wanted more; she wanted to prove to him that she could aim higher and wouldn't settle for less. There had always been a tension between them. I was proud of her, forging her way into the world of medicine which was still dominated by men.

So now I had much more time for myself, especially when Mac made further lengthy trips to South America. Rather than plunging myself back into voluntary work or church fundraising, I learnt to enjoy being on my own and to feel a deeper connection with myself; walking in the park, watching clouds, riding on a bus or curling up with a good book. And I continued to write in my journal.

Now, when Mac was at home, working in the EUSA office downstairs, I think he liked having me all to himself in the evenings. Over supper we would discuss whatever he'd been dealing with and gradually, instead of feeling resentful, I enjoyed becoming more involved with the day-to-day running of the office. I felt that I still had something to contribute to his work: typing his letters, filing documents or answering the telephone. I felt involved again. I belonged. In spite of our differences, Mac and I had reached some kind of mutual understanding. At last we were working together again, just as we had in the beginning, all those years ago in Cuzco.

And it didn't seem to matter that all the letters which I typed out for him, and posted to the missionaries in the field, were full of passages from the bible about having faith and trusting God – something I was still struggling with. I knew that what really helped those missionaries, was that when each of them read the letter which Mac had taken the trouble to write, they would feel connected and valued. And perhaps that's the best that any of us can hope for.

CHAPTER 19

London 1939-45

It's strange and slightly disturbing that as we grow older, the days, weeks and months all seem to fly past ever faster.

We remained in the house in Denmark Hill until the spring of '39 when Mac officially retired from his role as EUSA secretary. He was 66. Unofficially, he continued writing letters to the missionaries overseas, as well contributing regular articles to the monthly journal, *South America*. But the mission needed younger people in the office, so sadly, we moved to a small flat in Teddington. I had a yearning to return to my roots, somewhere peaceful, near to the parks and the river. Hampton was much too expensive but we moved as near as we could afford. We both agreed that it would be the last move we would ever have to make.

And then the war started.

Peggy had been in India since 1931 working in a school for blind children. It was a job she really loved. I was relieved to think that at least she'd be safe over there. Jean was now a qualified doctor, and when war was declared, she applied to the Royal Army Medical Core. Curiously they told her that they had enough doctors. I've always wondered if it was because she was a woman. Instead she took up a post in Obstetrics and Gynaecology in Plymouth.

Like everywhere else in England, Teddington was quiet and unaffected by the war for those first few months. But our peace was shattered the following autumn when German bombers made frequent raids. We spent many, many nights in the local authority shelters, listening to the noises outside, trying to remain optimistic on the surface while anxious about what we'd find when the raid was over. One of the worst attacks was at the end of November when bombs and incendiaries rained down all night, killing nearly one hundred people and reducing many homes to rubble. I couldn't believe that I was going to have to live through all this again. Mac, having missed so much of the Great War, now had a better appreciation of what we'd all gone through.

But for me, the spring of 1941 was the time I remember most. Plymouth hadn't suffered much damage up until then, apart from occasional air-raids on the docks. But in March, over two nights, the entire city was almost destroyed. Jean's hospital had a direct hit from a high explosive bomb and she was buried in debris and rubble right up to her neck. She was working in obstetrics, but on her ward there were also many sick children who'd been moved from the children's ward which had been damaged in an earlier raid.

It was pitch black, everyone was screaming and poor Jean couldn't even move her arms or legs which were trapped. After a while she heard footsteps and felt a boot kick her hard on her head. She tried to call out but her mouth was so full of dust she couldn't make a sound. Eventually someone shone a torch on her face, saw that she was alive and quickly dug her out. She was so brave. She had two broken ribs and a damaged foot, but as soon as she was pulled out from the rubble, refusing any further assistance, she made her way to where children's bodies were being laid out in a row and spent the rest of the night establishing which were alive and which were dead. Those who had survived she carried one by one to the adjoining maternity ward which was still relatively intact and tucked them into bed with the women patients until their needs could be tended to. Then she assisted a woman who'd gone into labour from the shock of the air-raid, dealt with numerous other casualties and finally went off-duty after twenty-two hours of solid work.

We read about the raid in the newspaper and I spent the next couple of days quite panic-stricken. We tried over and over to telephone her digs; not-knowing if Jeanie was alive or dead was quite unbearable. Eventually, a couple of days later she telephoned us and told us very calmly what had happened. She sounded exhausted and I kept having to ask her to repeat what she saying, because Mac was interrupting with questions of his own;

'Are you sure you are all right? Surely you can come and stay with us until you've recovered? That's ridiculous, Jean, they can't expect you to work if you've got broken ribs?'

But Jean insisted that she couldn't possibly take any time off when there was so much work to do. I was disappointed but so relieved she was safe. And I was very proud of my courageous daughter.

On November 4th, the day before my birthday, at

Buckingham Palace, the King presented Jean with the George Medal for bravery! The following year the Royal Army Medical Core were now delighted to accept her and although she was never near any fighting she did invaluable work in Hampshire and Yorkshire and even attained the rank of Major.

And Peggy, safely out in India? Not at all. In 1943, she caught diphtheria and had to be shipped home. She stayed with us in our tiny flat until she was fully recovered.

We thought we were secure but the dreadful bombing raids started all over again in 1944. The bombers were aiming for the National Physical Laboratory and the American army base in Bushey Park, but they missed both targets and hit innocent civilians, houses and shops. And then came the doodlebugs – a silent descent but an ear-splitting explosion on impact.

Somehow, throughout those awful years, our flat remained unscathed, but by the end of it all my nerves were in tatters. Mac, on the other hand, took a pragmatic approach.

'Come now Beatrice, you worry too much. We are both in our seventies and we've had a pretty good life, don't you think we can leave the rest up to God?'

CHAPTER 20

Teddington, London. Late August 1953

My life is being sorted into boxes. I must decide which parts to keep and which parts should be discarded forever. How on earth do I choose?

Already my small flat has been stripped. Peggy came last weekend. The walls are bare; only pale rectangles hold the memories of Lily's watercolours which hung there. The bookshelf, once bursting, gapes like an angry mouth. Several cardboard boxes are lined up near the door. Some of them contain things I will keep and some are destined for a jumble sale. Which is which? It's all a bit of a muddle.

Mac died in April after his second stroke, and both my girls are worried about me living on my own. So, I have reluctantly agreed to go and live with Jean's family in a large Georgian house in Hampshire which they have recently bought. Since her mother-in-law is moving in as well, and Jean is expecting her third child in November, she is keen for us all to be settled in before the baby comes. Having moved house so many times in my life, I suppose I should be used to it, but I'd really hoped I'd not have to move again. I know I should be grateful that she is giving me a home, and at least it will be in the countryside, but after the solitude of these past few months, I'm not really looking forward to it.

My task today, is to sort through my precious tapestry lidded chest. I can't remember everything it holds – it's quite a while since I opened it – but I do know that there are things in it which I might want to pass on to the next generation.

At the top of the chest is my beautiful pale grey alpaca shawl, last used to wrap Jean in when she was a baby. I press it to my face, smell the soft wool, and search for something long gone.

Underneath are more recent items; newspaper cuttings about Jean's George Medal, letters from Peggy when she was in India; an assortment of anonymous photos of various nieces and nephews; a rather battered bible. Further down still, there's a bundle of papers clipped together; school reports for the girls. "Margaret (no one called her "Peggy" at school) is hard-working and a joy to teach." "Jean loses concentration too easily and should learn to listen to what she is told."

How Jean will laugh when I show her these. If only we could go back and tell that teacher how wrong she was.

And here's a programme for school play; some faded stick-men drawings from when the girls were little; a matchbox with two tiny baby teeth; a rather squashed corn dolly.

Next is an envelope with all the letters Mac wrote to me, whenever he went away on one his trips back to South America. Tucked between them is a small piece of lined paper covered in a child's writing; it's the letter Jean wrote to us from Edinburgh when we were both away and she desperately wanted us to bring her back a parrot!

Another envelope is stuffed old photographs; me, in my awful missionary uniform; Mac, with his distinguished handlebar moustache; the steep narrow streets of Cuzco; Sacsayhuamán with its massive Inca walls; the beautiful snow-capped mountains; Indians in ponchos and woven skirts. But sadly, only a couple of my precious Monjaspata. Once I have moved, I am going to paste all these properly into an album.

Near the bottom of chest is the pamphlet that Mac and I wrote for him to use when he gave those fundraising lectures. "Our Nursing Work in Cuzco by Mrs A. Stuart McNairn, published by the Evangelical Union of South America." In just twelve pages, quite faded now, with accompanying photographs, it summarises the work I did out there, the dreadful conditions in which the women gave birth, and the absolute power that the priests had over every aspect of those poor women's lives. I'd quite forgotten the photograph of me on the first page. It was taken on my eighteenth birthday, before Papa died. My hair is pinned up, I have a pearl choker around my neck and I am wearing a lovely cream blouse with embroidered puffed sleeves. I think it was Mac's idea to demonstrate that once I was an apparently refined young lady who gave up everything to go and work with the poor women of Cuzco. He thought it would encourage people to donate more generously.

The chest is nearly empty now; the contents laid out on the table beside me. I sit in Mac's chair by the window, watching the pale-blue sky fade and the first dark clouds of night drift over the roof tops.

How glad I am that I have kept these treasures – these precious memories of my life. I hope that one day Jean will pass them on to her children, and it will be their turn to hold the threads which connect them with their past.

But not this last item. I lift out the small flat box, still tied with a pale blue ribbon, with Peter's flower posy presumably still inside. It is time to let him go – some of the past should stay in the past – and soon, a new baby, my last grandchild will be born.

It's getting dark. I make myself some toast and soup. Beside me, on the table are also some of the books that Mac wrote, which were published by EUSA. *The Lost Treasures of the Incas* by A. Stuart McNairn. Published in 1935, *Why South America?* Published in 1936, and his very last book, *Intercepted Letters* published just a month ago. It's such a shame he died before he saw the final version.

I never thought Mac would die before me. His funeral was a bit of an ordeal – so many people I knew and so many I didn't even recognize. I sincerely hope that I'll never have to attend any more. I've had quite enough of death. In the past dozen or so years, I've lost four of my brothers; Charles, Walter, Harry, dear Sidney and also my sister, Jessie. Susannah and I are the only ones left now.

But I think Mac would have loved his own funeral – all those speeches about what a wonderful man he was. It was good for Peggy and Jean to hear him spoken about so well. I hope Jean will remember the other side of her father, not just his moods and his stubborn need to be right. She always felt that he favoured Peggy over her and she tried so hard to prove that she was just as good. It was true. He was disappointed that she wasn't the son he longed for. And, of course, he didn't spend as much time with her as he had with Peggy, because he was so often working away from home.

Sometimes I worry about Peggy. She has spent her whole life looking after other people's children and never had any of her own. But she was never interested in young men and never married. I hope Jean will look out for her and make her feel part of her family.

I flick through this latest book, *Intercepted Letters*. It looks so fine with its dark blue cover and gold lettering. It contains fifty-two letters which Mac wrote over the years to various missionaries in South America. The editor persuaded Mac that the collection would make a little yearbook, with a message for each week. Although many of the letters are full of biblical quotations, there are several in which he reveals his more genuine and vulnerable side; the side of him I felt closer to.

I turn the pages until I get to Letter 44.

"Dear X, I am neither surprised nor shocked at all you tell me; for to be quite frank, you just describe experiences I have passed through again and again myself. In fact, I am afraid I am in just such a pit myself now, and it's a terrible snowy day! I only hope I haven't to slay a lion on top of it all, like Benaiah, for I don't feel equal to it. The truth is, you are passing through experiences and trials that the saints in all ages have been called to face – depression, discouragement, disappointment with yourself and with your progress, or lack of it, in your spiritual life... Believe me, my dear, these are symptoms of a complaint from which all children of God suffer if they are growing and not self-satisfyingly stagnating."

And in Letter 42 he showed how unafraid of death he was.

"Think not of <u>having</u> a soul and body, but instead of <u>being</u> a soul and having a body. Of course, we will all suffer death, but that is, after all, the heritage of man; it may even be terrible, painful – but it is only death; not a hair on your head, not an atom of the essential YOU, as God knows and loves you, will perish or come to any harm."

It's no wonder he was able to stay so calm when the bombs were raining down on us in Teddington.

At times I've envied his certainty about life, death and God, although even he admitted to having frequent wobbles. I remember him telling me that having an unquestioning faith in God would be like having the monotony of those long Andean months of sunshine, when we would begin to long for an English day of cloud and drizzle. But whenever Mac had his clouds of doubt he would return to the bible, and there he would find the words of encouragement and promise that he needed. He believed that he was loved by God. He belonged to God and after death he would be with God for eternity. And his sense of belonging was reinforced by his work as an essential member of the EUSA organisation.

But none of that really helped me. Over the years, I've grown to dislike the exclusiveness of organised religion and the blatant hypocrisy of many who call themselves Christians yet treat others with hatred or contempt. I don't want to belong to something that feels so wrong. I suppose I have felt a bit guilty about rejecting a belief, which at one time was so important, so vital. Part of me still feels bereft of the loving father-figure up in the sky who, as I'd taught the children, would take care of us forever, as long as were good.

But gradually, I have come to realise that perhaps it doesn't matter. Perhaps I don't need to understand everything or strive for some measure of certainty about God or the meaning of life. Tragic life events such as both World Wars, the death of children, and so on, no longer needed to be explained away as some sort of divine test. And having that burden lifted from me has been such a big relief.

What really matters is feeling connected – with myself, with others, with each day, with nature, music and our amazing world.

CHAPTER 21

Wickham, Hampshire. October 21ˢᵗ 1953

I have been here for almost two weeks. I am trying to put on a brave face but it doesn't feel like home yet. It's been such an upheaval. With all of us moving in at once, the house is still at sixes and sevens, but at least I have my own small bedroom upstairs which looks out over a shaggy lawn and gravel drive. I can't see the rest of the garden which stretches a good long way, but is completely overgrown.

Jean's husband, John, who is also a doctor, was a prisoner of war with the Japanese after the Fall of Singapore. Having a big garden was something he dreamt about and he whiled away the years in the camp making plans and sketches. There is to be a big vegetable patch and an orchard as well as a more formal section with a pond and raised beds. It sounds very ambitious and it will take a few years hard work yet to get it all planted. But I am glad Jean has married a man who likes gardening. I hope they will be good for each other.

I also have a sitting room to myself on the ground floor with two windows which look out onto a large square, lined with houses and shops on three sides. Apart from a

few parked cars and shoppers, it seems vast and empty –
not like the Plaza de Armas in Cuzco, always bustling with
life and colour.

The stairs will take a bit of getting used with my creaky
old hips. There is a wonderful polished wooden banister
which curls round at the first bend of the stairs and
again on the bottom step. It reminds me of the one in my
childhood home. Susannah and I were always being told
off by Nanny for sliding down from top to bottom! I'm
sure the grandchildren will love it. They are both delightful
but so noisy! Jillie is just over three and William is only
fifteen months. Poor Jillie was apparently most upset on
the day they moved in, because the large doll's house,
which she had seen when they were shown around by the
previous occupants, was no longer here. John, bless him,
has promised he will make one especially for her.

Unfortunately, I have to share both a bathroom and
a small dark kitchen with Jean's mother-in-law, Mrs
Campbell-Browne, as she calls herself. The only time I've
met her was at the wedding in '49, so I hardly know her.
She seems a bit frosty and I am not sure what to call her. I
am referred to as "Granny" and she is called "Grandmin"
– a reference to the fact that she and John for some reason
have always called each other "Min" – but it seems a little
too intimate a name for me to use.

From what Jean has told me, it sounds as if John's
mother had quite a difficult time in the war. She had no
news of her son for over nine months after the surrender
of Singapore and then she learnt that he was a prisoner.
And when it was all over and he returned safely, she'd
assumed that he would follow his original plan to become

a GP and come back to live with her in Lymington. It has clearly been a big upheaval for her to have to sell her house and move to Wickham. Apparently, she accepted that one day he would get married, but it seems that any wife he chose would always have to take second place. She has already established herself as the dominant matriarch of this household and makes frequent remarks about how Jean should be bringing up the children. With John being her only child, I am not sure why she thinks she can claim to be an expert in childcare!

Wickham, Hampshire. October 28th 1953

I go downstairs to make some tea and toast for my breakfast but seeing Mrs Campbell-Browne is in our kitchen, I retreat to the dining room where Jean is spooning porridge into William's mouth. He sits quite solemnly in his highchair and doesn't seem to notice my presence, his concentration fixed on the next mouthful. Jillie gives a squeak of pleasure as she sees me.

'Granny! Granny! Look my ribbon!' She pulls at the pale pink ribbon tied in a bow in her curly brown hair, and looks surprised when the bow comes undone.

'It's very pretty, Jillie,' I say.

'Mother. Do come and join us in here, for your breakfast.' She gives me a knowing look. I feel awkward. I'm still not sure where I fit in. I have my own rooms but am I supposed to keep to them or can I use any of the rooms in this rambling house? I don't want to intrude or be a nuisance. I don't want them to regret having me here.

Belonging or not seems to have been an issue for my entire life. I knew I belonged in our family when I was growing up, but then I lost that sense when Sidney and Susannah got married and we all went our separate ways. I felt totally accepted and part of the community at Doric Lodge until I went to Peru, where I struggled to feel included when we first arrived. Of course, once we had settled and I got to know everybody, I knew I belonged there. But then we had to leave and return to England and I had to start all over again. Even Mac found it hard to find his place in those early days after the war.

I suppose anyone can learn how to simply fit in; one just has to watch how others behave and then conform, even though that might mean putting on an act. But I don't want to just fit in with Jean's family. I want to feel that I belong here, though I dare say that will develop over time. We all need to get to know each other properly and accept each other, warts and all. I hope I can manage this with her mother-in-law.

I sink gratefully onto a chair beside my granddaughter who immediately clambers onto my lap. It's wonderful to feel the weight of a small child on my lap again. It's been an eternity since I last did this

Wickham, Hampshire. November 4ᵗʰ 1953

My birthday! I have reached the grand old age of seventy-eight. All day it has rained and I have felt rather marooned in the house. Now it is dark, the rain has stopped but the wind is rattling the window frames. Jean is resting, her ankles are a bit puffy and she is quite exhausted. We all wish this baby would get a move on; the tension is making everyone irritable. I worry that if it doesn't come soon she'll end up with a caesarean. John is downstairs with his mother, listening to a concert on the wireless which means I can sit with Jean in her bedroom and keep her company.

Earlier on when I came upstairs after my supper, I paused outside the children's bedroom. I could hear Jean singing to Jill; it was that lovely old waltz tune from the *Merry Widow* which I used to sing to her when she was just Jillie's age. It took me back to those early days of the war when Mac had gone back to South America and I used to sing her to sleep.

"If her eyes are blue as skies, that's my Jill. If her smile makes life worthwhile, that's my Jill. She's the sweetest darling I could ever know. She's my little girlie and I love her so."

It is lovely to see what a good mother Jean is. I wish I'd know mine. One of my biggest regrets is that I never asked my father anything at all about my mother. It was as if when she died any memory of her died as well. Her name was never mentioned, not even by my older siblings. It was as if the past had to be banished or forgotten, and it wasn't until I was ready to start a family of my own, that I realised that I had so many unanswered questions, and of course by then it was too late to ask. I suppose that when we are young and there is so much life ahead of us, we only want to look forwards and not back.

When Mac and I were young, working in Cuzco, we enjoyed looking towards the future and planning the next step. It's much the same right now for Jean and John; he has a new job, they have a new house and garden to sort out and their lovely children to bring up. Their future is bright and exciting. Before Mac had that terrible first stroke and lost his ability to speak, we used to love reminiscing together, keeping all our better memories alive. And now that I have nearly reached the end of my life, (not too soon I hope!) it's looking back that has given me so much pleasure; sorting through the treasures in my tapestry-lidded chest and showing them to Jean; weaving all the threads of my past together so that now she can carry them forward, blend them with her own, and one day, pass them on to her children.

Wickham, Hampshire, November 8th 1953

It's a girl! Alison Mary. 6 lbs and 8 oz. Born last night at 9.30 pm. Mother and daughter doing well!

What a relief. I can't wait to see them both. Hopefully they will be allowed home in a few days. It is a crisp autumn day and after all the rain we've had it is glorious to see a clear blue sky.

The first thought I had when John returned from the hospital last night with the news, was a wish that Mac could have lived to see his third grandchild. He would have cradled her in his arms just like he did with little Peggy all those years ago.

Wickham, Hampshire, November 12th 1953

Sun is streaming through the French windows. It catches the petals of the golden chrysanthemums which stand in a vase on the side table. William is upstairs having his nap while Jillie sits on the carpet at my feet, singing softly to her teddy bear. I try to concentrate on my knitting but I am so distracted, waiting for their arrival.

At last I hear the front door open. 'We're home!' Jean calls out.

'Mummy, Mummy!' Jillie scrambles to her feet.

We hurry to meet her in the hall. Looking tired but radiant, she walks towards me.

'Hello Mother, this is Alison, at long last. Would you like to hold her?'

I have waited so long for this moment. I pull the pale grey alpaca shawl from my shoulders, spread it over my outstretched arms and wrap it around my new granddaughter. Holding this little bundle of new life feels just perfect. I look into her dark brown eyes which gaze back at me. She gives a small snuffle of contentment and drifts off to sleep.

Arthur Stuart McNairn

Beatrice McNairn

[*Photo by Dr. E. T. Glenn*

The Mission House at Cuzco, " Monjaspata (Monk's Walk.)
San Pedro Church in the background.

Arthur Stuart McNairn

Beatrice McNairn

Jean with her parents 1941

Peggy with her parents 1941

AFTERWORD

My first novel, *The Mind's Garden*, was based on my father's and grandmother's World War Two experiences. Many who read it said they were intrigued to know what happened to John and his mother after the end of the novel.

Holding the Threads tells my maternal grandmother's story and that of my mother, Jean, whom John Garrett (Jesson) eventually married. It is not intended to be a biography, though the characters' names and the essential facts are all true. I have made some assumptions and have included some references which may not be completely true, but which I believe, help to set the scene in the historical context.

ACKNOWLEDGEMENTS

Much of the background and detailed descriptions for this book was made possible by documents made available by the Centre of World Christianity, Edinburgh.

Further detailed information was obtained from an invaluable source:
Peru: Its Story, People and Religion by Annie Geraldine Guinness. 1910. (Geraldine stayed with my grandparents while she visited Cuzco and this is recorded in her book.)

My Grandfather wrote many articles and books including:
Intercepted Letters by A. Stuart McNairn. 1953. Eusamerica
The Lost Treasures of the Incas by A. Stuart McNairn. 1935. Eusamerica
Do you Know? by A. Stuart McNairn. 1948. Eusamerica
Why South America by A. Stuart McNairn 1947. Eusamerica

Other sources include the following:
Cradle of Gold by Christopher Heaney. 2010. Pub: Palgrave Macmillan

Torn from the Nest by Matto de Turner. 1909. 1998 Oxford University Press.

Cusco Tales by Richard Nisbet. 2003. Publishing USA

Sons of the Moon by Henry Shukman. 1990. Weidenfield and Nicholson

Dawn Beyond the Andes by Phyllis Thompson. 1955. Regions Beyond Missionary Union

Three Letters from the Andes by Patrick Leigh Fermor. 1991. John Murray Publishers

Eight Feet in the Andes by Dervla Murphy. 1983. John Murray Publishers

Inca-Kola, A Traveller's Tales of Peru by Matthew Parish. 1990. Weidenfield and Nicholson

The Last days of the Incas by Kim Macqurrie. 2007. Piatkus Books

Turn Right at Machu Picchu by Mark Adams. 2012. Plume

Conquistadors by Michael Wood 2000. BBC Books

Exploration Fawcett by Col. P.H. Fawcett. 1953. Hutchinson.

Drumbeats that Changed the World by Joseph F Conley. 2000. William Carey Library.

Suffragettes by Gertrude Colmore, first published in 1910 as "Suffragette Sally", this edition published in 1984. Routledge Kegan Paul plc.